TWELVE STORIES IN ONE

GERALDINE McCAUGHREAN

A PACK OF LIES

Winner of the Carnegie Medal
and the
Guardian Children's Fiction Award

PENGUIN BOOKS
in association with Oxford University Press

PENGUIN BOOKS

Published by the Penguin Group
Penguin Books Ltd, 27 Wrights Lane, London W8 5TZ, England
Penguin Books USA Inc., 375 Hudson Street, New York, New York 10014, USA
Penguin Books Australia Ltd, Ringwood, Victoria, Australia
Penguin Books Canada Ltd, 10 Alcorn Avenue, Toronto, Ontario, Canada M4V 3B2
Penguin Books (NZ) Ltd, 182–190 Wairau Road, Auckland 10, New Zealand

Penguin Books Ltd, Registered Offices: Harmondsworth, Middlesex, England

First published by Oxford University Press 1988
Published in Penguin Books 1990
5 7 9 10 8 6 4

Printed in England by Clays Ltd, St Ives plc

for Teresa Heapy

CONTENTS

Chapter One	The Man who came from Reading	1
Chapter Two	The Clock: A Story of Superstition	11
Chapter Three	The Writing Box: The Story of a Liar	25
Chapter Four	The Plate: A Question of Values	41
Chapter Five	The Table: A Story of Gluttony	52
Chapter Six	The Harpsichord: A Story of Honour and Trust	60
Chapter Seven	The Umbrella-Stand: A Story of Temper	77
Chapter Eight	The Mirror: A Story of Vanity	90
Chapter Nine	The Roll-Top Desk: A Question of Whodunnit	104
Chapter Ten	The Wooden Chest: A Story of Betrayal	120
Chapter Eleven	The Lead Soldier: A Story of Pride	136
Chapter Twelve	The Bed: A Story of Horrors Unspeakable	148
Chapter Thirteen	The Only Answer	162

CHAPTER ONE

THE MAN WHO CAME FROM READING

She put down that she was interested in 'looking after animals' or 'heavy engineering'. But when it came to doing her fifth-year project on 'People at Work', somehow she got a half-day visit to the town library. It was like drawing the short straw. Nobody ever put down that they were interested in 'libraries', but someone was always sent there. The Head Librarian was kind enough to offer a visit for one person each year. So the school made sure to send someone polite; someone who would smile a lot and not say, 'But I put down Animals and Engineering.' Someone like Ailsa. The rude, loutish ones who said they were interested in 'bank robbery' and 'sex' (because to them that was witty) got a terrific day on the pig farm where they could not cause much trouble. And Ailsa got the town library.

She was shown the tickets. She was shown the large-print books. She was shown the newspapers and the telephone directories. She even read a story to a group of toddlers who sat and tore books to pieces at her feet. Around her the library echoed to the coughing of an old man reading *Windsurfing Monthly*, and to the scuffing, shambling tread of the public choosing books.

Success with Cactus Culture; *The Afghan War and its Implications for Trade, 1850–1900*; *The Collected Works of P. Edmund Grossmith*; *Double-Entry Bookkeeping in Guatemala*. Who read these books? Were there days when people rushed in from the street nursing a dying cactus, or woke longing to declaim from their balconies the verses of P. Edmund Grossmith? Was someone even now gazing out of an aeroplane bound for Guatemala wishing they had spent longer reading up on their double entry . . .

'Still raining, then?'

'Do you have anything by Catherine Cookson?'

'What weather!'

'Can you recommend something funny?'

'Raw cold, isn't it?'

'I'm sorry. The dog ate it.'

The voices came and went at the counter, while the rain hammered at the windows in an ecstasy of temper at being kept from so much fascinating reading.

'Now, as a special treat, Angela,' said the Deputy Librarian, 'you may use the microfiche machine!'

'Thank you very much, Mrs Millet,' said Ailsa.

'It's a kind of big magnifying glass, and these perspex sheets list all the books there are in the library, but in teeny tiny letters. Put them in here and – hey presto! – the words come up on the screen big enough to read. It's a bit like magic, isn't it?'

'Amazing, Mrs Millet,' said Ailsa politely.

'These letters here . . .' Mrs Millet went on, whispering as confidentially as any spy passing state secrets. The magnified green letters swam to and fro on the computer screen. When she was left alone, Ailsa inserted another microfiche, but the book titles skidded into view upside down and inside out.

Wisden Cricketers' Almanack 1956

She had it in the wrong way over. Ailsa yawned uncontrollably.

Suddenly a chin rested on her shoulder, and a mouth said into her ear, 'Leonardo da Vinci used to write like that, you know.'

Ailsa's hand jerked with fright, and the writing bolted

across the screen, blurring with speed. 'What, back-to-front?'

'No, on a computer microfiche. It's a little-known fact.'

She could see his grinning face reflected in the screen, with eighty-four titles in the series,

> Wisden Cricketers' Almanack 1955
> Wisden Cricketers' Almanack 1954
> Wisden Cricketers' Almanack 1953
> Wisden Cricketers' Almanack 1952
> Wisden Cricketers' Almanack 1951

superimposed in green across his features.

She eased her shoulder out from under his chin and turned to look at him properly, wondering if this was the kind of stranger she was supposed not to speak to. On the whole, she thought he was.

He had on a green corduroy jacket worn bald in all the creases of elbow, armpit and round the buttonholes, and an untied green bow tie snaked from under his collar. His white cricket flannels were colour-matched to his jacket by the long, oval grass stains on both knees. His suede shoes, too, were like a badly worn wicket, with a lot of dark, bare patches showing. His dark, curly hair had receded to that point which makes men look extra-intelligent and shows the veins in their foreheads when they are excited, and it curled directly into a short, dark beard which isolated his face from the paler skin in the open collar of his shirt.

'Like reading, do you?'

She shrugged. 'Fairly.'

'Fairly? Only fairly? Not unfairly? I like reading in bookshops – cover to cover – and then not paying. Are you on the Electoral Roll?'

'What?'

'Are you on the Voting List? They won't let me have any tickets here, because they say I'm not on the Voting List.'

'I'm not old enough to vote,' said Ailsa. 'But I expect my mother's on the Voting List. That's how I get tickets. I expect.'

His eyes lit up, and he seized her by both hands. '*You have tickets?* Can I borrow one? Or two? I'm in the middle of *Wisden's Cricketing Year Books*, and it's taken me three days to get to 1953, and it's not such a jolly place to spend the night, this, and I don't like to turn on the lights after hours in case some passing policeman mistakes me for a burglar.'

'You mean to say you've been . . .' But Ailsa did not have time to finish before the Deputy Librarian came round the bookshelves to quell the noise of raised voices.

She took one look at the man and hissed, 'You again! Look, I've told you until I'm tired of saying it – this is a place for quiet study or for the borrowing of books . . . Is he pestering you, Angela?'

'No, no,' said Ailsa and gave her polite smile.

'Look here, young man, where do you live? Why can't you go to your own local library? You've been hanging about here for days and days. Where are you from?'

'Reading,' said the young man, rather defensively.

'Berkshire?'

'Berkshire? If you like,' he said doubtfully.

'It is correctly pronounced *Reading*, to rhyme with "bedding", not *Reading* to rhyme with "breeding",' whispered the Librarian.

The young man narrowed his eyes at her. 'Who is it lives there, madam, you or me?'

The Librarian bridled. 'I'm going to ask you to leave now. Council bye-laws permit me to ask anyone to leave for whatever reason!'

His face fell. 'What? Turn me out?'

'*Shshsh!* Yes.'

'What? Like Adam and Eve turned out of the Garden of Eden by the Angel with the burning two-edged sword?'

Ailsa and the Librarian stared at him. 'Young gentleman, are you endeavouring to be funny?'

But he was not, for he suddenly fell on his grass-stained knees on the parquet flooring and grabbed the Librarian's skirt. 'Where could I go? It's winter! It's the football season! The cricket's gone till May! What would become of me?'

Mrs Millet's hands fluttered up around her shoulders, but she recovered fast and said, 'I'm going to call the Police now and have you forcibly removed.' She could not actually achieve this, because of the man clasping her knees, but as soon as he let go and turned his attentions to Ailsa, she was off like a rabbit, her crêpe-soled shoes squealing down the big, echoing room.

'*You'll* help me, won't you?' he cried, walking across to Ailsa on his knees. '*You* won't see me thrown out to wander the streets with nothing but traffic signs and graffiti to read and nowhere to lay my head at night! Where can I get a job? How can I get on to the Electoral Roll? I mean to say, *how can a fellow make a living*?'

'Our shop needs someone.' It had slipped out before Ailsa could prevent it.

'What kind of a shop? Whose shop? Where?'

'Second-hand furniture, mostly. My mother runs it. Dad died, and Mum's no good at selling anything.' There was a banging of doors at the end of the hall. 'Oh do get out of here before the Police come! They're only next door! *Please!*'

He nodded, got up off his knees and opened one of the big sash windows. 'I'll be waiting for you outside. Be quick. You're my salvation! You won't be sorry.' A blast of rainy air flapped the green corduroy as he climbed out through the window, and she could see the red stain where a cricket ball had been shined against his hip. She pulled the window shut behind him and sat down, trembling, at the microfiche. The Deputy Librarian and a policeman bustled into view.

'Here he is, officer . . . been hanging about here for three days now . . . oh! Has he gone, Angela?'

'Yes, Mrs Millet,' said Ailsa.

Upside down and inside out, the green screen blinked the words at her,

A Pack of Lies Oxford University Press 1988

And she thought she had been on the *W*s.

She considered creeping out some other way, but there wasn't one. There he sat, at four o'clock, on the concrete-slit bicycle-stand, and everything about him was a darker shade of green because he was so wet. Even his eyes seemed darker in the winter dusk. His suntan and beard dripped rainwater.

'You'd better come and talk to Mum,' she said doubtfully. 'I can't promise anything.'

'Fine! Fine!' he said, splattering through the puddles beside her as he practised his overarm bowling.

'What's your name? I ought to know it, to tell Mum.'

He answered without a moment's hesitation, 'Berkshire.'

'You're a liar, sir,' thought Ailsa. But nice, polite girls never say that kind of thing aloud. It is not in their upbringing.

'Oh Ailsa! You and your lame dogs!' was Mrs Povey's reaction to the news of a young man awaiting a job in the shop. She ran her fingers through her grey, permed hair, and her weary face forgot to repel all those lines of irritation and sadness that had settled there since Mr Povey's death. It had been a day spent worrying about money problems, with not enough trade in the shop to distract her attention from them. Now she stood dithering in the small, dark living room behind the shop, wondering whether she could send this young man away with a few sharp words, or whether she ought to be polite. She really did not have time to spare on being polite. But then this was the selfsame woman who had made Ailsa the girl she was. A woman brings up her children the way she was brought up herself, and politeness had run in the family for generations. It was like some dreadful hereditary defect. 'Well, I suppose I'd better have a word with this young man. Where did you leave him? What's his name?'

In the shop, Ailsa hesitated. She could not somehow bring herself to introduce the young man they found crouching behind a sideboard, rifling the second-hand bookshelves. But he grinned and reached up a large, dark-haired hand and shook Mrs Povey's vigorously. 'Berkshire's the name. MCC Berkshire. You didn't tell me there were *books*, Ailsa! Books!'

'Only second hand,' she murmured.

'Only? That's the best kind! My waking hours are entirely at your service, Mrs Povey!'

'Ah, well, I'm afraid . . . I think Ailsa doesn't quite understand the economics of running a little business like this. I'd certainly like someone to help . . .'

'And here I am! Fateful, isn't it?'

'. . . but I just don't see how I can afford to employ anyone, what with national insurance stamps and pension schemes and all the statutory things there are these days . . .'

'Oh, I'll work for nothing! Don't you worry about the money side. I haven't got any, either. Don't think another thing about it. A bite of lunch and free run of the books you've got in stock. Have you thought of opening up that side of the business? I'm good with books.'

'It's the furniture they come in for,' murmured Mrs Povey, looking sidelong at her daughter. 'Oh but this is nonsense. You can't work for nothing, Mr Berkshire. Nobody works for nothing.'

'It's better than walking the streets in this kind of

weather, but if you like, you can let me sleep on this. It'll save me paying rent somewhere.' He had run down the length of the shop and thrown himself on to a great creaking brass bed which rolled on its castors up against a chest of drawers. Whatnots and hat-stands were set rocking, and a stuffed parakeet swung on its perch, and an unwound clock chimed one. 'Think of the added security! Better than a burglar alarm any day.'

'Yes, yes, this is all very kind of you, Mr Berkshire,' said Mrs Povey, shaking her head, 'but are you really interested in selling furniture to people? Wouldn't you find it awfully *dull*, a person of your . . . your . . .' She was left struggling for an appropriate word.

'You mean, am I any good at selling things?' he said, making her blush with embarrassment. He got up off the bed and took both her hands in his and kissed them fervently. 'Put me on trial, madam! Don't make up your mind now. Try me for a week or two. I can sell things, don't you worry. After all . . . I sold myself to your daughter, and now even you are wavering on the brink . . .'

'Mother! I never really thought you'd take him on,' said Ailsa in disbelief, as they sat down to dinner that night. 'I thought you'd know how to tell him "no" in a nice way.'

Her mother sighed and signalled that Ailsa should speak more quietly, in case MCC Berkshire heard them in the shop below. 'I'm afraid young people get awfully desperate for a job these days. It didn't seem right just to send him away. He was so very *willing* . . . Such a good-looking boy, too,' she added vaguely.

'What's that got to do with it? He's weird.'

'Shsh, dear. Well, yes, he does seem a bit eccentric . . . or is he just *lively*? We're not very lively you know, we two.'

'We might be murdered in our beds, Mother!'

'Might we?'

'Oh Mother!' snapped Ailsa in exasperation.

Mrs Povey stirred her tea till it slopped over the rim of the cup. Her face crumpled into as many seams as a treasureless map. 'It's all very well for you, Ailsa. You start these things and you expect me to finish them. Eat your supper and don't nag, there's a good girl.'

They ate on in silence until the guilt felt equally shared again. Their eyes kept drifting towards the floor, as they both pictured the dark, cluttered shop below.

'He won't have eaten,' said Mrs Povey at last.

'No.'

'We ought to offer him some supper, I suppose.'

'It's only polite.'

For one hopeful moment Ailsa thought that MCC Berkshire had changed his mind and gone. The shop was a silent, unlit labyrinth of piled-up shadowy furniture, buttressed with bow-fronted chests and treacherous with reaching chair-legs and trailing electric flexes. Something moved, between the wardrobes and the leaf-fold tables, but it was only Ailsa's reflection moving in a big, old, gilt-framed mirror.

Then she caught sight of him perched at the top of a step-ladder by the bookshelves, the thin beam of a pencil-torch illuminating the cuffs of his white trousers. He did not seem to see her, for his face was sunk towards an open book on his lap and he was reading with all the still concentration of a mosquito sucking blood through a sleeping man's skin.

'You'll ruin your eyes like that,' said Ailsa, but he did not stir. 'Mother says, do you want some supper? It's only macaroni cheese.'

His eyes remained riveted to the page, but after half a minute or so he lifted one slow, absent-minded hand, to acknowledge that he had heard, and gave a kind of quiet moo.

'What does he say?' asked Mrs Povey, when Ailsa got back upstairs.

'He says "Hmmm". He's reading.'

So they waited, and grumbled, and watched the macaroni cheese congeal between them on the table. But MCC Berkshire never came for his supper. Not that night or any night.

CHAPTER TWO

THE CLOCK: A STORY OF SUPERSTITION

Next day, Ailsa was uneasy about leaving her mother alone in the shop with MCC Berkshire. But he seemed harmlessly engrossed in a book called *Furniture for the Amateur Collector.*

'I'm sorry we don't have anything more interesting,' she heard her mother say apologetically, and she shook her head in despair: Mrs Povey was no commander of men. That evening Ailsa hurried home from school and questioned her: 'Has he been a help? Is he good with the customers? Has he sold anything?'

Her mother smiled wanly. 'He's been no trouble at all. Really. He hasn't been under my feet or anything.'

Ailsa's suspicions were confirmed. 'He's read all day, hasn't he? He hasn't got up off that chair since I left this morning, has he? Be honest.'

'Well, he did have a cheese sandwich with me at lunchtime.'

'Oh Mother! He's going to be nothing but a drain on the cheese supplies. I've a good mind to tell him . . . he's got to go!'

'Oh yes, dear? You do that, then.' (She knew how to call Ailsa's bluff every time.) 'He says he's researching the subject – so that he knows about the furniture in the shop.'

'What's to know about it? It's junk furniture.'

'Ah no, MCC says there are some nice pieces in

among it all. And isn't it lucky that we had a book on the shelves about . . .'

'At least he'll go when he gets to the end of reading everything,' said Ailsa sourly. 'It's a good job we haven't got many books in stock.'

'Ah yes, well, this woman came in this morning with a whole suitcaseful of books . . .'

'And?'

'I told her we didn't deal much in books. And that I hadn't got much cash to spare at the moment.'

'And?'

'MCC gave her a credit note for £10 and took the books.'

'*Ten pounds?* Oh Mother!'

'Don't nag, Ailsa, there's a good girl.'

The next day was Saturday, and Ailsa was able to see at first hand the buzz of trade in action. It did not help that the newsagent next door had set up his ladder against his shop front, and that in their efforts to avoid walking under it, most passers-by walked out into the street and skirted Povey's Antiquary entirely. A couple came in at about 11 o'clock and said in loud voices how there was *not a thing* worth buying. A tramp came in to get warm for a while, because he knew Mrs Povey was always good for a cup of free tea. A schoolchild came in looking for a birthday present for its mother, and Mrs Povey pretended she had labelled a hand-mirror wrongly at a pound, and sold it to the child for ten pence. After the child was gone, certain nick-nacks were missing from the nick-nack table. An old man came in and knocked over a hat-stand so that it broke a china vase and chipped a wash-stand. And the milkman called, wanting to be paid.

All this while, MCC Berkshire lay like a cat along a green velvet *chaise longue* and read a book. One customer might have been interested in the *chaise longue* if it were not for the strange young man sprawled along it reading *Superstition and the Unexplained*.

At last, in the middle of the afternoon, a very pleasant, smiling major of a gentleman with a copy of the *Racing Times* tucked under one arm strode to the shop doorway, passing directly under the ladder outside. He went straight to a grandfather clock standing against the shop wall. He was obviously interested, judging from the animated way in which he stroked his soft, white moustache. Ailsa's heart rose. If only her mother would keep silent!

'This is a handsome timepiece. Yes indeed,' said the old gentleman.

'I'm afraid it's a bit big for most people's houses,' said Mrs Povey.

'Oh, but I've got one of those draughty old places with high ceilings,' said the old gentleman, fingering the shiny panels of polished wood.

'I'm afraid it doesn't keep time, though . . . in fact it doesn't go at all,' said Mrs Povey apologetically.

'Oh dear.' His face fell.

'The chains and things inside are all knotted up and broken.' She opened the front panel to show a heap of tangled, rusty hooks, chains and weights, and together they stood staring sadly at the disembowelled clock. 'I think it must have fallen over at some stage,' said Mrs Povey. 'You see the clock face is cracked, too.'

'Oh dear dear,' said the old gentleman, and turned away. 'What a pity.' Ailsa scowled at her mother's back.

'*Well, and won't you be telling him the story behind it, Mrs P?*' said a lilting voice from the other end of the shop. MCC Berkshire jumped up off the *chaise longue* and came down the room like a Grand National winner, leaping the furniture in his path. 'And won't you tell the man the story of how that fall came about?' he cried, rushing breathlessly to the clock and throwing one arm around its shoulders as if it were a cherished old friend.

'But I don't know . . .' began Mrs Povey, alarmed.

'Don't know? Well I do, madam, and it's a story that needs telling!'

'Mr Berkshire, I never knew you were . . .' But MCC had turned on the major.

'Now I don't suppose, sir, that you have the least interest in horses or the Sport of Kings, or you'd have heard of Lucky Finbar of Connemara.' He ran and pushed a moth-eaten winged armchair close up behind the major so that the old gentleman's knees were knocked from under him and he fell into it with a grunt. 'Well and maybe you wouldn't after all – him being born such a while ago and you such a young gentleman still in the eyes of history. Let me tell it to you the way it was, and you judge for yourself if there isn't a meaning and charm in the decline and fall of this clock.'

'Good God,' said the major, but he tucked his fingers together on the crown of his waistcoated stomach, sat back, and listened to the story MCC had to tell.

* * *

Before it came here, this clock was owned by an Irishman who had risen from stable boy to wealth thanks to a great talent for buying and racing horses. He won his first horse in a game of horseshoe-throwing with a jockey. The jockey should never have challenged Finbar to the contest: he had been drinking home-made whiskey since morning and could see three pins instead of just the one. Onlookers said it was no surprise he lost: he was too drunk to have hit the sea with a brick from a low-flying hot-air balloon. But Finbar saw things differently. He knew that Luck had smiled on him. Only that morning he had shaken hands with the seventh son of a seventh son, and that was why he had won himself a horse made of the very best horseflesh. He made certain of keeping on the right side of Luck after that.

He never missed Sunday Mass – unless he got out of

bed the wrong side by mistake and dared not leave the house for fear of bad luck. He always carried silver in his pocket so as to turn it over if he saw a new moon, and when one was due, he left all the windows of his cottage wide open, even in winter, for fear of glimpsing the new moon through glass.

Luck did not fail him. He won a multitude of races and acquired a string of horses, and any one of them fit to win the Dublin Gold Stakes. Of course, his success might have stemmed from living in Connemara, among the best horses in the world and the shrewdest horsemen in all Ireland, but Finbar knew differently. Luck was smiling on him.

So he always left something on his plate for the fairies, and he always said 'White Rabbits' on the first day of the month. His carpet wore a dandruff of salt, for he was forever throwing it over his left shoulder to blind any passing witches. Seeing him do this, Father Mulcahy asked if this were not 'a little on the pagan side'. But Finbar said there was no harm in being on the safe side. He wore more holy medals on his chest than a war veteran.

Luck was so kind to Finbar that he moved into a large house and could afford servants to keep it spick and span. But he fired the housemaid on the day she put his boots on the kitchen table to polish them. 'Don't you know that boots on the kitchen table are unlucky, you stupid girl!'

If he left a thing at home by mistake, he would never go back for it without turning round three times and sitting for ten minutes in the armchair. His house swarmed with black cats and (because he left the windows open at new moon) white cats and greys and tabbies, too. Cats will be cats, after all. And still good luck came to Finbar in plenty.

He planted yew trees in the garden, to fend off evil spirits, and banished all but lucky heather from his garden beds so that in spring they turned the colour of a bruise. He even took to drinking heather tea and poking sprigs of it into his horses' feeding net – though the horses spat it out which Finbar thought was a rather bad omen. He took to carrying a gun in case he saw any magpies on their own (which was bound to bring him sorrow). When Sergeant Yeats saw the gun he said it was a poor idea of Finbar's, but who can argue with a man who has just won the Connemara Four Mile Handicap?

Finbar was getting almost too good to hobnob with the likes of those at the County Fair. But he had started feeding a new mare of his on nothing but lucky heather, and he wanted a chance to try her out in a race. So he entered the County Races. When the local bookies saw that Finbar was riding in the afternoon, they packed up their suitcases and went home – for everyone liked a bet on Lucky Finbar and Lucky Finbar never lost.

But the leprechauns (or perhaps it was the heather) made the mare fractious. No sooner did Finbar mount up and the toe of his boot touch the mare's swollen belly, than she took off in a string of great bucks and leaps, bit a steward, and bolted towards the starter's chair.

Now at the Connemara County Fair in those days, the starter used to start the races sitting on the top rung of a whitewashed step-ladder. It was a very tall step-ladder, but not as tall as the starter would have liked when he saw Finbar's mare pounding towards him, neck outstretched, teeth bared, eyes rolling. He drew up his legs and blew his starter's whistle and wagged his flag, but it only seemed to madden the horse even more, for she put her head down and charged like a bull at a toreador.

If Finbar had seen what was coming, he would most surely have hurled himself out of the saddle on to the turf. But all he expected was to be slightly maimed against the starter's chair. He did not foresee how the mare – groaning as only a horse which has stomach-ache can groan – would duck beneath the A-frame of the ladder and try to carry the starter off, like an elephant under a howdah. Finbar flattened himself along her neck. The starter passed by overhead . . . and they were safely out the other side, with nobody even scathed. The mare galloped herself to exhaustion, then rolled over on her side and lay foaming at the mouth, looking as bloated and glassy eyed as Father Mulcahy after his Christmas dinner.

As Finbar walked back the way he had unwillingly come, he saw the dreadful truth of the situation. The starter was still clinging, dazed, to the top of his chair, like a look-out on the mast of a foundering ship. The chair itself cast a dark arrow of a shadow which seemed to pierce Finbar to the heart. *For it was a ladder!*

Had he not passed beneath a ladder – the unluckiest act of them all? Would not all the misfortunes of Heaven rain down now on his unprotected head? A sweat broke out on Finbar that washed all the colour from his face for evermore.

'Maybe it's not really a ladder in the true sense of the word,' he told himself. But even as the hopeful thought passed through his head, the owner of the starting chair came out of the crowd and began shouting, 'That's the last time I lend me ladder for such purposes! I hope me ladder's come to no harm. 'Tis me best ladder, too, and me tallest, and I thank God 'twas tall enough on the day!'

'Ah shut your misbegotten mouth,' yelled Finbar, to the man's astonishment. 'I'm a ruined man for sure!'

It might have been better if Finbar had sat back and waited for bad luck to crush him. But it preyed on his mind very greatly, and he could not decide finally whether a step-ladder being used as a starter's chair was indeed a starter's chair or a step-ladder. Besides, he felt a need to know what particular shape his bad luck would take when it came. Would it be injury, horse-flu, bankruptcy, a losing streak, robbery . . . or worse?

So when he saw the advertisement in the *Connemara Chronicle* which said:

ASK GYPSY JO PAIDRIC
WHAT'S IN STORE:
HE KNOWS MORE!

he was quick to follow its advice. He put on his best suit, and caught the train to Ballymuchtie where Gypsy Jo Paidric the Clairvoyant had a small consulting room over a fish shop.

Now anyone on the superstitious side might think it meaningful that Finbar happened upon that particular advertisement and that particular gentleman. Paidric Conlan had become a gypsy shortly after his betting shop closed down. A bankrupt man must make a living where he can, and there was no-one so thoroughly bankrupt as Paidric Conlan the day after the Dublin Gold Stakes.

He got by now by telling young ladies they were in line for handsome husbands, and telling mothers that their babies would grow up into great men. He gave some delight. He did no harm. There was no malice in him. Not much, anyway.

White-faced with worry, Finbar threw himself down in the chair opposite Conlan and bared his soul. 'In my past, sir, people knew me as Lucky Finbar, and I'll be the first to admit that Luck has smiled on me since the first day I was born.' He paused.

The gypsy clairvoyant had dropped his pipe into his lap and was in a fever to brush the burning tobacco off his trousers. Paidric straightened his headscarf and breathed deeply: there was a lot of colour in his cheeks. 'I've heard tell of you, now I think about it. Lucky Finbar? Yes. Didn't you have a great deal of the winning kind of luck in the Dublin Gold Stakes a couple of years back? Do go on, sir.'

'Well, I believe I've done a dreadful thing – bad

enough to dent my luck all out of shape and let the leprechauns in to plague me. I . . . I passed under . . . a ladder!' And he recounted the fearful events of that terrible day, while Paidric sat staring at the ceiling and shuffling a deck of playing cards.

'Deal the cards for me, Finbar, and I'll tell you the worst,' he said.

Finbar dealt a rather jolly pattern of red cards all over the table-top. Gypsy Paidric sucked his teeth and said, 'Try it again, sir. I don't like the look of it.'

Finbar dealt again. Paidric shook his head and rolled his eyes. 'There's no softening the blow, sir. You'll be dead before the year's out, and that's a racing certainty.'

Finbar's eyes bulged and he clutched at his hair. 'D . . . d . . . dead? Is there nothing I can do? It wasn't all that much of a ladder at all, you know?'

'Who can cheat his fate?' said Paidric stoically, and packed his cards away and opened the door to let his customer out. 'That will be ten shillings, sir.'

When Finbar had gone – stumbling down the stairs like a milk bottle kicked off the step – the clairvoyant bared his teeth in a bitter grin and muttered, '*Revenge!*' If it hadn't been for that fluke string of winners at the Dublin Gold Stakes meeting (and all of them ridden or owned by Lucky Finbar, the bastard) Paidric Conlan would not have been cleaned out, ruined. Only once in a generation does a bookie get as unlucky as that. If it were not for Lucky Finbar, Paidric Conlan should have been a rich man now instead of pretending to be a gypsy in a one-room hole over a fish shop.

On the way home, Finbar found the world had turned vicious all of a sudden. Every hurrying horse-drawn cab, every lout lounging on the street corners, might suddenly turn murderer. On the return journey, he fully expected the train to hurl itself off the rails, or the rivers to rise up and drown him. Trees shook their branches at him menacingly, and roof slates lay in wait, ready to throw themselves at his head and brain him. He counted thirteen magpies roosting in his garden before he could get his key to turn in the lock and could rush indoors into the sanctuary of his fine big house.

And who should be standing in the hall to greet him but the great, walnut grandfather clock, his one-time pride and joy. It gazed down at him, the hands standing at ten-to-two like a smug grin. *Tock tock tock.* The sound of it filled the quiet house, picking off the seconds, one by one, of Finbar's remaining life.

He fired his cook, for fear she poison him. He fired his manservant, for fear he was secretly a notorious murderer. He fired the housekeeper, because she said he was 'a mad old fool of a superstitious pagan to go wasting good money on clairvoyants in fish shops.'

He boarded up the windows, for fear of a sudden outbreak of war or revolution. He shot the skirting-board into splinters, thinking the mice might bring plague into the house. 'I defy it! I defy my fate!' he told the ever-watching clock, but its face made no change of expression.

Days came and days went, and Finbar, though he made himself sick with worry, did not die. In fact, being a jockey, he was exceptionally fit. Of course, he never left the house to ride now. It was far too dangerous to go out. Anyway, a horse might throw him or bite him or trample him or roll on him . . . so he shouted through the letter-box that his neighbours must shoot the horses, one and all. His neighbours helped themselves to the horses of their choice and trotted cheerfully away, saying, 'It's lucky for us that Finbar's brain has finally fallen off its hinges!'

November came, and December, and the bookies at all the race-tracks grew fat and wealthy, because Lucky Finbar was no longer racing.

Father Mulcahy called often at the house to ask if Finbar wouldn't go to Sunday Mass.

'No!' screamed Finbar through the letter-box. 'You only wish to sell me a plot in the churchyard, but I'll not be needing one, I tell you! I'll not be needing one!' And Father Mulcahy went away again, quite baffled, shrugging his shoulders and pulling weeds out of the garden path.

The clock in the hall ticked on relentlessly, picking off the minutes like a sniper.

All the fun of Christmas took everyone's minds off the strange change in their neighbour Finbar. In fact they forgot all about him, sealed up in his big house. All the company he had was the big clock in the hall: *tock tock tock.*

The circular sweep of its hands swept todays into yesterdays, Christmas Day into Boxing Day, Boxing Day into New Year's Eve.

'Dead before the year is out. *Tock tock tock tock*' – and then a clamorous burst of tinny laughter as the chimes cracked another hour over the head. Finbar opened the walnut door in the front and bawled at the pendulum, 'The gypsy was a liar! I'm not going to die!'

But the pendulum simply wagged a stern finger, and the clock said, '*Tock tock tock tock*: Dead before the year is out.'

The noise dropped on Finbar like the waterdrops that wear away a stone. They cut him like those thousand cuts by which the Chinese Emperor used to kill his prisoners. *Tock tock tock tock.*

The noise of partying carried from the village on the wind. Midnight and the end of the old year was approaching, second by second by second. *Tock tock tock tock tock.* The New Year could be heard coming closer and closer . . . its footsteps echoed round the hall: *tock tock tock tock tock.*

Terror gripped Finbar by the knees and tumbled him into a basket chair, from where he stared up at the clock-face. His heart was beating so hard that he perfectly believed it would fail him before the clock struck midnight. What reason did the gypsy have to lie? As the mystical man had said, what man can escape his Fate? *Tock tock tock tock tock.* Five minutes remained of the year, and Finbar must die before the year was out.

'Who's to say what year it is?' Finbar demanded of the clock. ' 'Tis only the likes of you that drives one year out and the next one in. If it weren't for clocks we could live inside of one year all our lives and pay no heed to time passing. What's Time, after all? Eh?' (The clock did not reply except to say, '*Tock tock tock tock tock.*') 'Didn't a mere man invent it in the first place? Didn't we divide things up and give 'em the names "seconds" and "minutes" and "hours"? If we made it, we can do without it! Time's a thing entirely invented by the sellers of birthday cards and Christmas presents *and clocks*! . . . Why that's it, after all! Time was only invented by clockmakers, and 'tis only kept by clocks! Well, I'll have none of it in my house! I'll none of it, see! I'll put a stop to your murderous tick-tocking! You shan't count me out like some old boxer on the canvas!'

It was one minute to midnight.

Dragging the basket chair to the foot of the clock, Finbar turfed out the cushions and climbed up. A heavier man would have put his feet through the wickerwork, but Finbar was a jockey and as light as a whippet. He fumbled at the fastenings of the glass clock-face, and it flew open just as the chain-strung mechanism heaved up its chain like a ship weighing anchor. There was a click and a whirring of springs. Finbar put his finger to the minute hand and forced it backwards.

(Foolish man. He need only have stopped the pendulum.)

The chime mechanism was already triggered. It clanked and churned, and the whole frame juddered. Face to face with the staring dial, Finbar felt the noise of the first chime like a punch on the nose. He reeled sideways, caught his ear on the catch of the clock-face, and snatched his head away in pain.

The basket chair, unnerved by his curses, slid away from beneath him so that Finbar was pitched forward and embraced the great jarring shoulders of the chiming clock. The clock swayed forwards eagerly. Its door fell open, its chain and pendulum and rods and counter-weights and chimes spilled out. Fatally wounded, the grandfather clock crashed down on its face.

Beneath it lay a few wicker twigs – the remnants of the basket chair – and Lucky Finbar, terror of the bookies, darling of the fairies – and the most super-stitious old fool in the history of all Ireland.

When it all came out, Paidric Conlan the Clairvoyant was a made man. He counted it the greatest stroke of luck that he had correctly predicted the dreadful fate of poor, dead, Lucky Finbar.

* * *

By the time Mr Berkshire had finished, Ailsa was sitting on the wash-stand with her mouth dangling open. Mrs Povey, stricken with embarrassment, had backed down the shop towards the rear exit and was wringing her hands desolately. The major was crouched forwards in the armchair with his chin on the head of his walking stick, gazing at the clock and grinning.

'I'll take it, by God! What're you asking, boy?'

'A hundred, sir, and may it bring you good luck.'

'I don't know about luck, you young – er – but it's brought me the best morning's entertainment since General Patton got trod on by the regimental drum-mer's horse. Send it round this afternoon and be sure all the bits and pieces are inside. I'll have it restrung. Be good as new. Capital clock. Capital story. Capital!'

When he had gone, Mr Berkshire wiped his hands down his jacket and beamed. 'That's the way to sell a thing,' he said with massive satisfaction.

'*But it was all lies*,' whispered Mrs Povey, there being no polite way to put it.

MCC Berkshire drew himself up to his full six foot and more. '*Lies*, madam?'

'Well, er . . . yes, actually . . . Lies.'

'Not *lies*, madam,' he declared, magnificently unrepentant. '*Fiction*. That's the thing to give 'em. That's the thing everyone wants. *Fiction, madam!*' Then he loped back towards the *chaise longue*. As he passed Ailsa he nudged her with his elbow, winked, and gave her a quick, brilliant smile. 'Sold it, though, didn't I, eh?'

'Certainly did,' she said, backing off a step or two. 'You're not Irish at all, are you, Mr Berkshire?'

'Not that I know of,' he said with a blithe shrug, 'but you never can tell for certain.' And he plunged heavily on to the green velvet and into his book once more. 'And do call me MCC. Please.'

CHAPTER THREE

THE WRITING BOX: THE STORY OF A LIAR

MCC Berkshire seemed to have gone out, even before breakfast. But Ailsa and her mother noticed that the ladder had been moved from outside the newsagent's next door, and stood against the lintel over their own front door. Ailsa ran outside and saw that the dingy, peeling lettering of 'Povey's Antiquary' had been smartly touched up. And the words 'DEALER IN BOOKS' had been blocked in, small, on the last half-metre.

'How very kind,' said Mrs Povey. 'I wonder where Mr Berkshire is. I must thank him.'

'I wonder if he asked permission to use the paint or the ladder,' said Ailsa sceptically, and moved it all back to the front of the shop next door. She was only just in time, for as she reached her own doorway again, their Indian neighbour, Mr Singh, came out and noticed the theft of his bicycle.

He was a man who had never been heard to swear. But from the way he kicked over the shop's litter bin and jumped on the empty cartons that spilled out, Ailsa thought he was probably rather attached to the bike. He was, in any case, too upset to notice that his ladder and paints had been interfered with.

'I've been thinking about what Mr Berkshire said,' observed her mother, gazing raptly at a raised spoonful of breakfast cereal. 'He didn't exactly say that our clock was *the* clock in the story, you know.'

'Didn't he?'

'No – and the customer didn't really believe him, anyway.'

'Didn't he? Isn't it a lie, then, if it isn't believable?'

'Goodness, Ailsa, you can be pompous when you set your mind to it. I can't think where you get it from . . . I mean, it's perfectly true that the clock will be fine when it's restrung . . . and it was a fair price, taking that into consideration.' Her face flushed with pleasure at the thought of the money. 'I'll be able to pay the electricity bill now,' she said dreamily, as if that had always been her fondest ambition.

'Er . . . Mother.'

'Yes dear, I know I owe you pocket money, too.'

'No, it's not that . . . exactly where is the money? The old man paid cash, didn't he?'

Mrs Povey did not turn pale all at once. Her hands went to her apron pocket, and then her eyes wandered to the mantelpiece, the biscuit tin, her handbag, and all the other places she might have put a hundred pounds for safety. Her arms mimed the exchange of payment: 'I remember seeing the old gentleman count the money into Mr Berkshire's hand . . .'

'Now don't panic, Mother,' said Ailsa, her chair scraping the kitchen floor. 'You telephone the police and I'll see if anyone in the street saw which way he went!' They collided in the doorway and fought each other on the stairs. Mrs Povey knocked the telephone off its stand and Ailsa became entangled with a length of plastic potted plant. By the time she had extricated herself and opened the shop door, she was certain she knew who had stolen Mr Singh's bicycle, and where her mother's hundred pounds had found a place of safety. But what to do? Which way to run? If MCC Berkshire had left while they slept, he could be in the next county by now.

She rammed heavily into Mr Singh who was standing on the edge of the kerb, pointing up the street. Down the crown of the road came MCC Berkshire on the stolen green bicycle. He was wearing a white pith helmet, such as Englishmen wore to hunt tigers in the days of the British Empire. He was reading a book propped open on the handlebars. The panniers of the bike were crammed to overspilling with books, and under one arm he carried a large wooden box, lacquered so that it flashed in the light. So engrossed was he in the book that he almost overshot the shop, and had to scuff one shoe noisily along the tarmac to turn and pull up.

'So dreadfully sorry for the removal of your transport, sir,' he said, thrusting his box into Mr Singh's outstretched, accusing hand, and handing the book to Ailsa while he dismounted. He spoke with a very clipped precision, as if English were a foreign language he had learned to perfection. 'It was most necessary that I should reach the railway sidings in time for the very first car boot to open.'

'Mr Berkshire, where's the money from the clock?' said Ailsa.

MCC placed the bicycle with infinite care against the lamp-post and refastened the combination padlock. He unpacked the books from the panniers as if he were Securicor making a delivery of gold bullion, loading them into the arms of Ailsa and Mr Singh until they were buckling at the knees. Then he put an arm each round their shoulders – being considerably taller than either of them – and led them conspiratorially into Povey's Antiquary. 'You see there was this Car Boot Sale and Flea Market advertised and if you can get to these things right at the start there are some real bargains to be picked up. Take that box, sir. That, sir, is a genuine Victorian writing case – rosewood inlaid with cherry. Not veneer, mind! All handcrafted inlay work. And all it's short of is a key.'

Mr Singh, who was being quickly off-loaded by Mrs Povey, was soon left holding only the box. He tried to open the lid. 'But it's locked shut!' he protested.

'Yes, think of it! Think of the secrets that box will keep till the day of its destruction!' cried MCC, snatching it out of his arms.

'It's useless!' insisted Mr Singh excitedly, tugging it back and rattling it. 'What use is a box you cannot open, if you will be so good as to tell me?'

'You're a Utilitarian, sir!' said MCC, snatching it back.

'I'm a Sikh, sir!'

'But you think a thing is beautiful only if it's useful. You are a Utilitarian!'

'Mr Berkshire! Mr Singh! Please!' begged Mrs Povey. 'Have some coffee! Have some breakfast!'

'I have newspapers to sell, Mrs Povey, madam. But if I were you, madam, I wouldn't trust this kind of a fellow, with his bicycle-stealing and his foolish hat and his *suntan*! No no. Where has he been for such a suntan, I ask you, while poor people like us are working to earn a living?'

A look of shocked injury crossed Berkshire's face, and his eyes, under the brim of the pith helmet, were darker than the Ganges river. '*And must I apologize for having Anglo-Indian blood?*'

Mr Singh did not know which way to look. He was covered with embarrassment. He stroked one sleeve of the green corduroy jacket soothingly. 'My dear young gentleman! I, who have so often had abuse in my own shop, to my own face, about the colour of my skin! That I should cast insults on a man partly of my own race! Now I look at you, of course I can see that your eyes are . . . I'm glad you . . . borrowed my bicycle, yes certainly. I am very glad. And now I come to look, it is indeed a very fine box. What craftsmanship! It is for Mrs Povey's excellent establishment to sell, I suppose?'

'Ah yes, and what a story it has to it!' exclaimed MCC, and Ailsa made a snatch at his hand and dragged him aside – almost into a giant, mirrored wardrobe.

'Please, Mr Berkshire,' she whispered, feeling the

whole weight of the family business resting on her shoulders. 'Please don't tell Mr Singh any *more* lies. He's a nice man. And he has a bit of a temper. And he only lives next door.'

'*More* lies?' said MCC, loudly astonished. 'What lies have I told?' And when she looked up into those wide-open, long-lashed eyes, they were indeed dark enough to be . . . 'It's odd. Your mother mistook me for a liar yesterday,' he continued, in a loud voice. 'Now I could tell you a story about a liar-and-a-half in connection with a certain wooden writing box.'

He eased out past Ailsa, despite her protesting hands on his chest, and she was left with the sensation that she had just touched something still connected to the mains electricity. When she rounded the wardrobe, Mr Singh was perched up on a second-hand bar stool, wearing the look of a snake confronted with a snake-charmer, and MCC had started his story.

* * *

Dearest Mamma,
I hope you are well. I hope Papa is well. The weather here is v. vile. We have not got out in the park for days. Last week was Easter in the church. The minster said we must forgive those who spitefully use us. But it is v. hard. Belinda steals out of my trunk and Sarah puts mice in my bed and Miss Stubbs has such favourites, truly! I think some mammas and papas must send extra money so that Miss Stubbs will be nice to their girls. I wish I was in India with you and Papa. I would v. much like to see India now that us British have made it sivvilised.
Miss Stubbs says it is v. educational and I miss you so much, dearest Mamma. And dear Papa, too.

Grace Briavel-Tomson sucked the end of her pen, and stared out at the rain-shiny street. Her fingers drummed on the sloping lid of her beautiful escritoire. She knew how much her mother liked to get letters from her. She was under strict instructions to write every week. It was hard to think of enough things to write *every* week. It was different for her mamma and papa. Life in India was so very interesting, with fakirs and opium and bazaars and typhoid and army balls and skirmishes with the natives and child brides and widows being burned on funeral pyres. Kensington was very dull by comparison. In India, a girl would have native servants to do everything for her, and hunters risking life and limb to shoot tigers and lay the skins at her feet.

'They ought to send for me,' she thought, watching the ink well up into the nib of her pen like a big blue teardrop. 'They *shall* send for me! Why should they enjoy themselves out there at all those dances and polo matches, and leave me sitting here learning stupid French? It's not fair! Well it's not.'

She chewed ferociously on the end of her pen until inspiration came, like milk through a straw, and she scribbled off a last few lines to fill the sheet of pink paper.

> *Matron uses some very strange language, Mamma, and calls Peter the caretaker a 'bastard' and a 'sot'. Could you kindly tell me what these words mean as I do not understand them. Your afectionate and loving daughter asks God to bless you –*
> *Grace.*
> *PS Please send a little money if you can spare it, for Morgana twisted my arm and pulled my hair until I gave her all my pocket money, and I fear v. much that I shall have nothing to put in the collection plate on Sundays.*

As she blotted dry her letter and addressed the envelope, she called out in a shrill, piercing voice, 'Morgana! Where are you?'

A timid, gangling girl hurried clumsily into the room, all hands and feet and apologies.

'Take this letter to the post, Morgana.'

'Oh, but Grace! It's raining so *hard*!' whispered the girl pleadingly.

'Take it! . . . Or do you want me to pull your hair again, like before? Oh and you'll have to go to the Post Office for a stamp, first.'

'But Grace! You took all my . . . I mean you borrowed all my money. Don't you remember?'

Snatching hold of the girl's white lawn smock, Grace wiped her inky nib on its ruffles before laying the pen neatly in its compartment and locking her escritoire with its little silver key. 'Then you shall have to borrow the money from someone, won't you, dear?' she said sneeringly. And when Morgana had left the room, crying, Grace muttered, 'Silly bastard,' and ate some of the cake she had stolen from Belinda's trunk.

To her great vexation, Grace's letter did not have the desired effect. Her mamma was suitably horrified to discover that she had placed her dearest daughter in such a den of wickedness. But instead of sending a liner ticket by return of post, she arranged for Grace to live with an elderly aunt in Knightsbridge, and advertised in *The Times* for a governess.

This was a great deal worse than Kensington Preparatory School for the Daughters of the Empire. There was no-one to persecute, no-one to pay for her expensive little pleasures, no-one she could frighten into doing her schoolwork. The governess, Miss Starch, was a harmless enough woman with a round, homely face and a box of toffees in her desk drawer to give Grace if she were good. The box came out often, but regrettably Grace rarely deserved the toffees she was given. Being good was not Grace Briavel-Tomson's chief ambition in life.

Miss Starch was a Methodist and played the harmonium at the Methodist Chapel on Thursdays. Late at night, by the light of a spirit-lamp, she liked to write little songs of praise for her fellow-worshippers to sing. Miss Starch was flattered that Grace always wanted to see her hymns and to copy them out . . . but then she did not know how useful they were to Grace for her weekly letters to India:

Dearest Mamma, I thought you might like to see a few lines I wrote this week. They just came into my head from nowhere. I hope you like the words. I am sorry I am not in India. Then you could hear the tune, as well.

Grace's mamma collected quite a treasury of verses in this way, and cherished them lovingly in a leather-bound book labelled, 'Gracie's Poems'.

Sometimes, a particularly handsome young Methodist would walk Miss Starch home from the Thursday service. It was seeing them stand together in the lamplight beneath Grace's bedroom window which gave her the idea of how she still might get to India.

Dearest Mamma and Papa,
It is my v. painful duty to tell you that Miss Starch is not so respectable as she seems. Last night I saw her kissing the telegraph boy, and this morning she was holding hands with the baker. Aunt Gladys says Miss Starch is 'carrying on' with a Methodist, but I don't know what that means. People say she writes coarse music-hall songs as well, for sixpence a time, but I don't think this can be true, because she is always trying to borrow money from me. Do please let me come to India. I don't like to be here with Miss Starch and Aunt Gladys – especially when Aunty is drinking the gin.

This did the trick. Before the month was out, money was telegraphed from India to pay for a liner ticket to Bombay. Miss Starch was fired without notice, without explanation, and without references. Her young man broke off their engagement for fear of scandal touching the Methodist Chapel of Knightsbridge. Aunt Gladys was deeply hurt that none of her puzzled letters to India were answered: there was not so much as a Christmas card – only a small pamphlet all about the dangers of strong drink. This startled Aunt Gladys, who was a lifelong teetotaller.

India sweltered under a sky the colour of bruises. The air was thick with flies. A rain of mosquitoes and blowflies beat into her face, and the light hurt her eyes. At night, the dark leaned on her as if exhausted by the heat, and the undergrowth hummed with the promise of huge, grotesque insects. It was true that there were servants and ayahs to do everything Grace told them. But Grace took an immediate dislike to her personal ayah.

Raissa had hair so long, glossy, thick and beautiful, that she deserved to be hated. She was fabulously lovely, and looked so precisely like the princess in Grace's favourite story-book, that Grace learned to hate the book as well.

Raissa, like Miss Starch, was betrothed, but of this Grace was not envious. For the servant girl was promised to a sun-wizened little man who moved about the house on bare feet, as silent as villainy. Sometimes he seemed to be watching his betters with those liquid brown eyes . . . in fact, whenever Grace looked around. His name was Imrat, and he rode a green bicycle without a bell, whose brakes bound on the wheel rims with a strange shush-shush-shushing. It was a sound Grace came to associate with a shiver down her spine and a tightening in her throat.

'When I was in England, I had six butlers and three personal maids and a carriage to take me anywhere I wanted to go,' she told Raissa (to put her in her place).

'When I was in England I had this also,' said Raissa.

'Oh! When were *you* ever in England?' exclaimed Grace.

'I was never in England, Missy Sahib,' said Raissa, and slipped out of the room on her silent brown feet.

Grace sent Raissa on the long walk into town almost every day to buy lengths of cloth in the bazaar. When Raissa brought the cloth, Grace would say, '*That*'s not the kind I meant at all.' 'I said red, not blue, you stupid girl. Take it back and get me my money! Now! This instant!' But often, when Raissa had gone, Grace would hear the shush-shush-shushing of the green bicycle and knew that the girl was riding pillion down to the town, which spoiled the whole thing.

'I believe I shall take you tiger-hunting and use you for bait,' said Grace, hoping to frighten the girl, for she had heard that the natives were all stupid and gullible.

'I fear there is a great shortage of tigers this season, Missy Sahib,' said Raissa, bowing. 'Rats there are in plenty, but they feed where they choose.' And for a week, Grace's dreams swarmed with big brown rats, and her imagination filled the darkness outside the bungalow with gnawing and squealing.

Raissa must go. Grace quickly reached that conclusion. But she was patient, and waited her chance. The perfect opportunity came the evening after the Embassy Ball, when her mamma's few items of jewellery were still lying where she had taken them off, not locked away in Papa's deed-box.

Grace looked around once, looked around twice, and swept the jewellery into her smock pocket. She would hide it in Raissa's bedding when there was a chance to enter the servants' quarters unseen. In the mean time, she hid the booty where she had once hidden the things she stole at school – in her beautiful escritoire.

It was there when she went to sleep that night, sweltering under her mosquito net, pressing her fingers into her ears to block out the pitiless throb and whirr of the tropical night.

Of course, as she slept, her hands fell away from her ears. She became aware, in the darkest hour before morning, of a soft shush-shush-shushing which brought her suddenly, unaccountably wide awake. The moon was bright. It silhouetted a host of winged insects crawling, crawling, crawling on the white mosquito net. They were just like the pictures she had seen of angels hovering over a death bed. Grace pulled the covers over her head and howled with rage that her parents should have brought her to this horrible, sweating country.

In the morning, at breakfast, she waited for the dreadful news to break – that Mamma's jewels had been stolen. Not a word was said. How very unobservant Mamma must be! She had not even missed her jewels. Grace hurried from the table at the end of the meal and went to her mamma's bedroom. The jewels lay exactly as they had lain after the dance.

Was she mad! Had she dreamt the whole brilliant plot and performed none of it? She ran to the escritoire. It was empty. The innocent pink stationery blushed up at her, ashamed.

'You have not lost something, Missy Sahib?' Raissa said, creeping into the room on her silent brown feet.

'No! Go away! Get out!' yelled the young English gentlewoman, stamping her feet in a tantrum.

Next day, her mamma and papa went away to tour the province. Grace was left alone in the silent house which reeked so of flowers and sunlight and the servants' meals of curry. She was speechless with resentment and boredom, and scuffed through the rooms, glowering at the caged birds, the ivory statuettes, the sun-bleached magnificence of the carpets on the walls.

How she longed to go walking in the rain amid the noise of horse-drawn cabs and the smell of soot and rainy newspapers, under the flicker of gas-lamps and a murky, English sky. Around her, the entire Indian subcontinent stretched out like an ocean on which she had been cast adrift. Instead of seagulls, there were vultures; and instead of fish there were lizards, and instead of sharks there were dark, sinister figures in crisp white clothes riding green bicycles with binding brakes . . .

'Raissa come here!' Her voice was so shrill that the caged macaw out on the verandah answered it with a shriek.

Quick and smiling and eager to please, Raissa appeared from nowhere on her soft feet, the hair spilling from a half-wound plait like dark wine pouring down. She bowed with all the grace of a white crane, her palms pressed together as though she were holding a butterfly captive between them. 'You called, Missy Sahib?'

'Yes, Raissa. Why were you so long? Fetch me some big scissors.'

The scissors came with no clattering of drawers or turning out of boxes.

'Now sit down, girl. I'm going to cut your hair.'

'No, Missy Sahib!' The slim brown hands flew to the plait. 'Why for?'

'Because I would like a hairpiece made of it – and because if you don't give it me I'll find someone else to be my servant. While my papa and mamma are away, I am the mistress of this house. So sit down and let me cut off your hair!'

Raissa looked to right and left, like a fawn scenting a tiger. 'I go now to the town and buy you hair, Missy Sahib – plenty beautiful hair – much more beautifuller than mine.'

Grace put a weary fracture into her voice. 'Oh dear, Raissa, you are very vain. Didn't you know, it's a sin to be vain?' Grace pounced. Her serving-girl, though she might have held out for justice at the hands of the master and mistress, though she might have forfeited her job rather than her hair, *dared* not fight hand-to-hand with an English gentlewoman. Besides, Grace was strong and well-practised in torment. She was armed, too, with a long pair of very sharp scissors.

For her part, Grace, drunk on the adrenalin pumping through her brain, sobered a little when she felt the hair in her hand. There would be a price to pay when her parents returned. They were always saying that servants should be treated with respect, and they showed signs of being fond of Raissa. Sometimes Grace thought they showed Raissa more affection than her . . . All these things went through her head as she knotted her fist in the rope of black hair. And perhaps fear of the consequences made her hand waver, for she slashed the plait across half-way down its length, and left enough of the silken black to cover Raissa's face as she broke free and fled from the room.

There was something vile and half-alive about the hank of hair Grace was left holding. She ran to her escritoire and pushed the hair inside, under the tray. It left a smell on her hand of safflower oil, that would not come off with washing.

That night, the crickets and toads roared round the house like a migraine, and the moonlight plastered it with sweat, and the flickering shadows of bats flecked the moonbeams as thickly as motes in sunshine. Fireflies were setting a slow fuse to the world, and when it burned right down, there would come an explosion of Papa's anger. Grace lay awake, trying to think of a lie that would get her out of trouble.

'I know! I found Raissa stealing one of my dresses and cut off her hair as a punishment. They'll take my word against hers! They're bound to!' Grace allowed her backbone to relax into the mattress and the darkness to reach up for her . . .

She must have dozed for a few moments, for she dreamt she heard a mechanical shush-shush-shushing and the ping ping ping of a broken spoke against a mudguard. She sprang awake, her scalp prickling with unease.

Perhaps a letter to her parents might be a wise precaution. Otherwise Raissa's clever tongue might win

Papa round before Grace had a chance to banish the girl from their affections. Yes, a letter. Perhaps then Papa would *write*, dismissing the girl, and it would never come down to Raissa's word against hers. 'How fine a thing is a good education,' thought Grace, slipping out of bed. 'I doubt if that girl can even write her own name, let alone write letters like mine!' And she lit a lamp which drove the darkness away to a safer distance.

Through the house she went, waking the macaw and the monkey with the light, but no-one else. The whining of insects seemed to beat against the house and make it tremble, but after all, it was only the flicker of the lamplight that made everything quake. She composed in her head as she went.

Dear Mamma and Papa,

Do send word that that dreadful girl Raissa be dismissed. This morning I found her wearing one of my dresses . . . and cutting her hair *with my needlework scissors! When I remonstrated with her, she said 'I'm as good as you any day' and wanted me to curl her hair to look like me. I think she is only behaving like this because you are away, but oh, dear, precious Mamma, I simply don't know how to handle servants, and she does frighten me so with that little penknife of hers. Darling Papa! Did you know that her betrothed – the man called Imrat – is a Nationalist and wants to 'wash the English out of India on a tide of blood'? Such people! Do please write and advise me what must be done. I am so very alone without my dear Mamma and Papa . . .*

Flushed with the thrill of inspiration, she pulled her escritoire to the edge of the table, drew up a chair, opened the lid, and lifted out the tray of pens. As she reached in for the paper, something soft and cold curled around her wrist and gave her a fright. Then she laughed at her foolishness. 'Of course! Raissa's plait!'

She drew out the pink stationery and shook her arm to dislodge the rope of hair.

But it would not shake off. In fact it clung tighter, taking another turn and another around her forearm, the bulbous end searching up inside the sleeve of her nightdress . . .

Until the snake struck, Grace was still convinced that the blackness round her arm was nothing more than a hairpiece cold with safflower oil. Afterwards, she just had time to hear – beyond the cackle of the macaw and the jibbering of the monkey and the migraine roar of the Indian night – the shush-shush-shushing of brakes binding, as a bicycle rode away across the lawns. Then the poison stopped her pulse – for a vein runs direct from the right hand to the heart.

* * *

By this time, the pavement outside the shop was full of forlorn, irritable people, craning their necks this way and that for the owner of the empty newsagent's. They clutched large Sunday newspapers and palms full of coins. Mr Singh left at the run to serve them, but returned ten minutes later, carrying a black tin cash-box.

'If you would be so good, I should like to buy the delightful wooden writing box, Mrs Povey. And there was a book also that I saw . . . a book about India and the days of the British rule.' (It was the book MCC had had propped open on the handlebars, and he fetched it instantly.)

'Oh Mr Singh, I couldn't . . .' said Mrs Povey.

MCC held out the box and the book, and the newsagent's arms closed around them as the arms of India once closed around her sweet Independence.

'But the box has no key!' said Mrs Povey sadly.

Mr Singh hugged it closer to his chest.

'Oh but Mr Singh, it's Sunday and I shouldn't . . .'

Ailsa crossed to the mantelpiece behind Mr Singh and held up the red electricity bill behind his shoulder so that it was in plain view of her mother.

'Well, if you'd really like it, I'm sure Mr Berkshire can tell you how much it's worth.'

MCC took the electricity bill out of Ailsa's hands and read off it unhesitatingly, 'Forty-three pounds thirty pence, including VAT.'

As the shop door was pulled to behind Mr Singh, Ailsa said to MCC Berkshire, 'How did you know the combination on Mr Singh's bicycle padlock?'

'Guessed it,' said MCC unswervingly, as he tossed the pith helmet on to a hat-stand.

'You must have done.'

And there she left it. For, after all, there was no other explanation.

CHAPTER FOUR

THE PLATE: A QUESTION OF VALUES

Of the hundred pounds nothing remained. Other larger purchases MCC Berkshire had made at the car boot sale and flea market arrived later in the day: a set of bookshelves and a stuffed salmon in a glass case. The little shop seemed to groan at the prospect of swallowing yet more indigestible junk, and if it had not been for the sale of the clock, the bookshelves would never have found a piece of wall to lean their backs against.

Mrs Povey said to her daughter, 'Maybe he's right to open up the book side of the business.'

But when a teacher from Ailsa's school came in one day and thumbed his way through the fiction, he was brought gradually to a halt and a shiver by the feeling that someone was watching him. He looked up, and found MCC Berkshire standing a word's length away from him, scowling. The teacher rummaged for his wallet. But MCC said, 'I haven't read those yet,' and prised the books out of the customer's hand. 'I've been saving the fiction, you see.'

'Ah! Quite!' exclaimed the teacher, and turned tail and fled, casting a look of bewildered pity at Ailsa and Mrs Povey. (The word got about school after that, that Ailsa had a strange, deranged brother at home and that he was the reason the shop was in such dire financial trouble.)

'*That*'s how to sell a thing,' said Ailsa sarcastically,

when her teacher was gone. Then Berkshire looked down at the books cradled against his stomach and stroked the spines with his fingers and seemed too ashamed to speak. And Ailsa wished she had kept silent, and wondered what had possessed her to be so rude. 'It doesn't matter,' she said. 'Books don't pay enough to make any difference. They're not worth anything. Mum sells them for pennies, second-hand books.'

'Some are worth hundreds!' said MCC, perking up.

'We don't have any like that.'

'It's all a question of values,' he said, appraising his new bookshelves, full of dilapidated paperbacks, and his eyes when he said it were as deep as Chancery, full of glints of gold from the lamplight. 'Money isn't everything.'

The sky outside was almost black with rain and every car that went by had its lamps switched on. With a loud crack, a thundercloud broke overhead. Two lovers, joined at the hands like Siamese twins, came bursting into the shop, laughing, and shaking off the rain. It was plain they had dashed into the first handy shelter and had no intention of buying.

'Oh, this is pretty . . . Oo, look at that dear little vase . . . what a pity this has lost its lid,' said the girl from time to time. But her boyfriend was only watching for the rain to go off. She picked up a little book of Chinese folk tales lying open on the *chaise longue*. When she lifted her eyes from browsing through it, she found herself being watched, from the dark recesses of the shop, by a young man.

MCC pressed the palms of his hands together and bowed from the waist. He moved silently round the *chaise longue* and took the book out of her hands as if to read its title. 'Ah! You are interested in ancient China, then!' She recoiled in alarm. 'In that case, permit me to draw your attention to this charming plate.'

'Oh look, Brian! What a pretty plate!' cried the girl, dubiously. MCC slyly slipped the book into his pocket.

Brian came and looked at the blue and white plate balanced between two urns. 'Oh yeah. Willow Pattern. Your Gran's got a whole service like it. Is that the only one?'

It was the only one – and even so, Ailsa could not remember seeing it before, though she knew the kind of thing. Well, the Willow Pattern is a common enough design.

'Is it old?' asked the girl, looking for a price.

'The story is,' said MCC Berkshire.

* * *

Long ago, in China, during the Ch'ing dynasty and the days of the Manchu Emperor Ch'ien Lung, there lived a potter called Ho Pa. He was a mean, greedy and spiteful man. But he had an apprentice working for him whose work was so perfect that people called from far and near to buy porcelain at Ho Pa's pottery. Ho Pa grew very rich indeed. But he did not pay any of the money to the apprentice, Wa Fan, who did all the work. Instead, he cursed and cuffed the young man and made his life miserable and called his pottery worthless and ugly.

If only Wa Fan had known! His beautiful vases and plates and teapots and dishes were bought even by the Emperor's Court! And travellers from far distant lands paid huge sums to sail away with just one piece of Wa Fan's craftsmanship. One pattern they asked for more often than any other. 'Give us Willow-Pattern plates, Ho Pa! We will pay you extra if you make us Willow-Pattern china in blue and white!'

Then Ho Pa would stick his head round the door of the hot, wet pottery and shout, 'Willow Pattern, Wa Fan! Give me more Willow Pattern, you idle son of a sleeping dog!'

Wa Fan did not mind. The Willow Pattern is a very beautiful pattern and tells the love story of a boy and a girl and a garden, and Wa Fan delighted in painting (in blue glaze with a very fine brush) the pretty garden with its bridge and pagodas. He painted petals on to the chrysanthemums with such care that the flowers seemed to be alive. He painted the figures so beautifully that their clothes seemed to billow in the breeze.

Sometimes – on the best days of all – his master's daughter, Liu, would come into the pottery and talk to him about his work and admire the china drying on the racks. She never tired of hearing Wa Fan tell her the story of the Willow Pattern, as she pointed out each detail in turn.

'And who is this?' she would ask (although she already knew).

'That is the cruel father,' said Wa Fan. 'A rich merchant who will not let his lovely daughter marry the gardener.'

'And this is the lovely daughter?' Liu would say, (although, of course, she already knew). 'And this is the poor gardener? What became of the unhappy lovers?'

'The daughter and the gardener loved each other so much that they decided to run away together into the world outside the garden. They hid in the gardens – all night, the delicate lady hid in a spidery, dark shed. But the cruel father discovered their secret and searched the garden at dawn. The only way out was over the lake, across a narrow bridge. When the lovers came out of hiding and made to leave the garden, there on the bridge stood the cruel father, whip in hand, ready to kill the poor young gardener. When the lovers saw that it was impossible to escape, they jumped off the bridge, thinking to drown together in the lake.'

Then Liu would come bursting into his story and exclaim, 'But the gods smiled on them and turned them into bluebirds, and they flew away to lasting happiness!'

Then Wa Fan said, 'You know my story already,' and Liu blushed and covered her mouth with her fingers and trotted to the door on her wooden heels and clattered back to her father's house.

You see Liu loved Wa Fan the potter, and Wa Fan loved her. But they could no more hope to be married than a fish can hope to fly.

One day cruel Ho Pa said to his daughter, 'You may thank me, Liu. Prepare yourself. Whiten your face and redden your lips and dress your hair with flowers. For I have found you a husband.'

Liu bowed low to her father. 'I will indeed thank you, father, if the husband you have chosen is Wa Fan, your apprentice. He is a fine man.'

'*Who?*' cried Ho Pa. 'Ha! Do you suppose I would marry a daughter of mine to a worthless apprentice? No! You shall marry Chu Fat, the merchant, whose wealth is as huge as his belly and whose business sense is as quick as his temper and whose reputation is almost as old as he. He shall sell my pottery, and together we shall grow richer than the Emperor himself. You shall marry tomorrow. Speak no more of Wa Fan.'

Liu said nothing. In old China, during the Ch'ing dynasty and in the days of the Manchu Emperor Ch'ien Lung, a daughter's words were worth less than dead leaves blowing down a street. But the birds of sadness pecked at her heart.

In those days, Ho Pa rarely went to his pottery, for he had Wa Fan to do all his work and Wa Fan's china was finer than anything Ho Pa could ever make with his own hands. Now he went straight there, and walked up and down the racks, pretending to examine the plates and vases and bowls.

'Tell me, Wa Fan, what do you think of my daughter?' he asked casually. He saw the apprentice's hand tremble as he painted the leaves on to a blue willow tree.

'She is the pattern of all beauty, master; a creation more perfect than any vase shaped by hand, any words written by poets, any music sung by minstrels.'

'And what would you say if I told you you could marry her?'

Wa Fan dropped his paintbrush altogether and leapt

up from his stool. 'I would say that you are the best of men and that I am the happiest!'

Then Ho Pa held his sides and laughed till the tears ran down his fat cheeks. 'Hear this, you shineless pebble on a dusty road: my daughter will be married tomorrow to Chu Fat, the merchant, and I shall stop your wages for daring to rest your eyes upon *my* daughter! Ha! ha! ha! What do you say to that?'

Wa Fan said nothing. For in old China, during the Ch'ing dynasty and in the days of the Manchu Emperor Ch'ien Lung, the words of an apprentice were worth less than the ants in a spadeful of earth. But inwardly the dogs of sadness chewed on his heart.

'Some token of respect – some present for the happy pair – would be acceptable,' said Ho Pa, sweeping out of the door.

Wa Fan went to the window and looked out at the splendid gardens which surrounded Ho Pa's still more splendid house. The orange blossom was tearful with rain. The willow tree by the lake slumped with rounded shoulders. The lake glimmered through the reeds like teardrops on the lashes of a great sad eye. Wa Fan looked for a long time at the little bridge hunched over the lake. Then he fetched a plain, undecorated plate of finest pottery and glazed it white as milk, and then began to paint, in a glaze as blue as purple, one last Willow-Pattern story.

It was work more perfect than any Wa Fan had ever done before.

He baked the plate in the kiln and the figures and flowers stood out so brightly that they seemed to move across the little bridge beside the ornamental lake and the painted pagodas. In them the fate of Wa Fan was fastened. He could not turn back now.

On the morning of the wedding, Wa Fan went to the market and bought strawberries, and heaped them on the plate and dredged them with sugar, and took them to the door of the great house where his master lived.

Bowing very low to the doorkeeper, he said, 'Please set this miserable and worthless present before the bride and groom, and say that it is a token of respect from the insignificant Wa Fan, apprentice.'

The contracts had been signed. Liu sat at table beside the gross and wheezing Chu Fat – like a golden carp beside a whale. The tasselled rods and flowered combs fastening her hair trembled, and her eyes were fixed on her lap. Her father sat at the head of the table, drinking toasts to himself and his ancestors in cups of rice wine, and laughing immoderately.

The doorkeeper brought in a plate of strawberries and set it down between the bride and groom. 'A token of respect from the insignificant Wa Fan, apprentice.' Liu started a little, and her father let out a roar of laughter big enough to fill a ship's sail. The bridegroom plunged a fat hand in among the strawberries and crammed twenty into his food-clogged mouth.

Liu rested her gaze on the blue rim of the plate. She had no eyes for the strawberries. She loved Wa Fan, and so she loved to look at his beautiful craftsmanship. She smiled sadly to see the picture emerge from beneath the strawberries as her betrothed crammed the fruit into his face.

No-one saw her shoulders stiffen, her eyes grow wide, or her fingers crumple the edge of the tablecloth. For during the Ch'ing dynasty, in the days of the Manchu Emperor Ch'ien Lung, a woman learned to be silent and unnoticeable in the eyes of men. She took one strawberry from the plate. And then another.

She was not mistaken. Her own face looked up at her from the blue and white garden of the Willow Pattern. She it was, who stood on the bridge hand in hand with the poor gardener.

Another strawberry.

And there was her father – there was Ho Pa in every shape and feature, standing on the bridge. There was his angry scowl, his vain heap of hair, his big fist grasping the whip, his twisted mouth swearing vengeance.

Another strawberry and oh!

Who was it who stood hand in hand with her on the legendary bridge but Wa Fan, the apprentice, dressed in gardener's clothes but quite unmistakable to the eyes of one who loved him. A perfect self-portrait.

The plate was a message. The plate was a letter, a plea, a proposal. The plate said, 'Run away with me, Liu, for I love you as the gardener loved the rich merchant's daughter in the Willow-Pattern story.'

Liu's lips parted and she said, so silently that only her ancestors heard her, 'Yes, yes, Wa Fan. I will come.'

'Pass those strawberries to me, daughter, or have you no respect for your father?'

Liu's heart fluttered between her ribs like a bird caught in a trap. The faces on the plate were showing clearly now. Wa Fan's plan was laid bare. It was there for everyone to see. Would Wa Fan not pay for his daring with life itself?

'Daughter! Bring me the plate!'

She could not disobey. She carried the plate to her father and he ate the remaining strawberries. Only a snow of sugar still rested on the blue and white shining garden of the Willow Pattern.

Ho Pa picked it up and examined it. 'I see Wa Fan has done his finest work for my daughter's wedding gift.'

But though he looked at the cruel and raging face of the man on the bridge, he did not recognize himself. For Ho Pa was vain and he thought himself handsome. He did not recognize the face of the girl on the bridge, for he had never cared enough to look closely into her face. And he did not recognize the face of his apprentice, for he had never looked upon Wa Fan as a man, only as a pair of hands which earned him money: a tool, an object, a thing. He turned to his daughter and said, 'Fetch more strawberries. The plate is empty.'

He handed it into her hands – Wa Fan's priceless wedding gift into her hands. He sent her from the room when all she had lacked was an excuse to leave the room. Along the corridor she hurried, holding the plate to her breast – out into the garden where the sun shone smilingly, past the chrysanthemums, the painted pagoda, and along the lake shore to the little bridge. There, hidden among the tresses of the willow tree, she found Wa Fan, his long pigtail held anxiously between his nervous fingers.

'You came,' he said.

'I came,' she said.

'You have left behind everything for me,' he said.

'I have left behind nothing,' she said, 'for look, I have the present you sent me and that is all in the world that I prize. I will never part with it.'

Then they crossed over the hunched little bridge, hand in hand, and into the world beyond.

They went to the harbour, and there they found a Portuguese merchant ship making ready to sail.

'Carry us to your faraway land in the West,' said Wa Fan to the Portuguese captain.

The captain – a swarthy man, fearful to Chinese eyes with his coarse-bearded jaw and big moist eyes – looked at the ragged Wa Fan and at Liu in her wedding dress. He plucked at his lip. He looked in vain for their luggage. 'And how will you pay me, Chinaman?'

'With hard work and thanks,' said Wa Fan.

'Oh many, many thanks,' said Liu.

But the sea captain's heart was as cold and sharp-pointed as the anchor of his ship. It lay like a moneybag within his chest and its purse-strings were pulled tight. 'I vouch some father will pay me well for the return of his daughter,' he said, twirling his dark moustache. 'Some bridegroom will pay me well for the return of his bride.'

'No, no!' cried Liu, covering her face.

'No, no!' cried Wa Fan, shielding her with his arm. And the sea gaped, and the waves gasped, the topsail shook in the wind.

Then the captain saw the plate which Liu held to her

breast. His eyes gleamed and his hands could not help but reach for it. 'Did you say you had no fare? This is Willow-Pattern china from the pottery of Ho Pa and the finest piece I ever saw. This will pay your fare!'

He snatched at the plate, he fumbled, and the delicate porcelain fell between ship and dockside. It floated on the water like a lily.

Into the water leapt Wa Fan and seized the plate and held it high over his head, and the sea captain snatched it – more precious to him than a child – from its watery destruction.

'Wait!' said Wa Fan struggling ashore. 'The plate does not belong to me!'

The captain turned, scowling. 'What's that? Is it stolen?'

'No, indeed! But it is the property of this lady, and only she may give it away!'

Liu looked long at the beautiful plate dripping between the sea captain's hands. At last she said, 'What is china compared with the fate of two hearts? What is a plate compared with the face of my Wa Fan? What is a thing made with hands, compared with the hands which made it?'

So Wa Fan and Liu set sail across a tangle of foam, towards the shores of distant Europe. Their souls were so filled with invisible joy as to fly like two birds above the ship, whiter than the flapping sail.

Meanwhile, the sea captain kept below decks and gloated over a thing moulded from clay and painted with the colours of crushed flowers. He thought the plate a rich addition to his cargo. But there are those who believe he had aboard his ship a far greater treasure.

* * *

'Oh Brian!' said the girl.

'Oh Traycie!' said the boy.

'Oh buy it for me, Brian!'

'Don't be daft. It must be worth hundreds.'

'Not necessarily,' said MCC, and his eyes were as deep and dark as the South China seas but quite empty of sharks. 'Value doesn't always show itself in the price.'

Brian groped a handful of coins out of his jeans, and Ailsa wrapped the plate in tissue paper. She meant to scratch off any disappointing, tell-tale English pottery mark on the back, but there wasn't one. There was only a long, dangling, Chinese cipher shaped like a chain of paper lanterns.

'Where's the sweet little book?' wondered Traycie, searching about in the region of the *chaise longue*.

'What book's that?' said MCC, resting his hand in the pocket of his green corduroy jacket.

CHAPTER FIVE

THE TABLE: A STORY OF GLUTTONY

On the first Saturday in every month, there were Sales at the Auction Rooms in Bridge Street. Ailsa and her mother had not been there for some time, because the shop never sold enough to need restocking. But after MCC had been with them for a month, spaces opened up between the crowded furniture, like the gaps in a grandstand towards the end of a day's cricket. There was little to show for it in the till, for as soon as he made a sale, MCC was off shopping for books and yet more books. Still, MCC insisted they went today to the Auction Rooms.

'But I don't have any money to spend at an auction!' protested Mrs Povey, as Berkshire held out her coat to her.

'Speculate to accumulate. You've got to invest to survive. You've got to spend if you want to earn!'

'You've been reading the economics books again, MCC,' said Ailsa, and wondered why her mother had given in. They had no money to spend on new stock: they couldn't even afford to pay the telephone bill.

'Who'll start me off at five pounds for this genuine reproduction samovar?' asked the auctioneer.

The central heating was not on in the Auction Rooms, and a huddle of shivering, grumbling dealers sat hunched over typed lists of the things for sale. MCC said, 'Why doesn't anyone bid? It's a nice samovar. It reminds me of my Great-Uncle Alexei who once got his troika stuck in a snowdrift and lived on tea for three days.' Cointantaneously, Mrs Povey and Ailsa (who were sitting on either side of him) took hold of MCC's hands to stop him bidding. He looked down in astonishment, squeezed their hands, and said, 'How nice. Thank you.'

There was a ship's wheel, a garden hose, a wardrobe, a half-made rug kit, assorted china, a broken scooter, a wheelchair, two dead aspidistras in pots, a sideboard, a fireguard, a fridge and a stuffed ferret. The dealers liked the sideboard and the china, but would not bid at all for the rest, though MCC's hands twitched hungrily. 'I knew a man once who owned a laundrette and trained a ferret to fetch out all the socks and handkerchiefs that got stuck in the machines.'

'Did it work?' asked Ailsa, tightening her grip.

'Almost. It fetched them out every time. But it ate them.'

The auctioneer scowled at MCC and said, 'Did I hear a bid, sir?'

'No!' squeaked Mrs Povey.

It was nearing lunchtime. The dealers got out their sandwiches, with a rustle of cellophane and paper bags. As they did so, a huge table was brought up on to the dais: a vast, polished mahogany oval as shiny and reflective as a village pond and almost as big. The dealers stirred in their seats and their frosty breath sprang up in a dozen plumes of admiration. Even Mrs Povey said, 'Now *there*'s a lovely piece,' and absent-mindedly let go of MCC's left hand. She was dizzy at the sound of the spiralling bids – three hundred, four hundred, five hundred, five-fifty . . .

'Seven hundred pounds!' declared MCC, lifting his right hand as if Ailsa were no more than a handkerchief tucked in his cuff. Suddenly there were no more bids.

Mrs Povey burst into tears. 'No bid! No bid!' she tried to call, but it became all tangled with the tears and the shivering and the scraping of chairs as the dealers turned in their seats to identify the bidder.

'Now are you happy?' said Ailsa.

'What's the matter?' MCC asked, hurriedly passing Mrs Povey his silk handkerchief.

'Going once at seven hundred,' said the auctioneer.

'We don't have it!' hissed Ailsa.

'But it's worth much more than seven hundred,' argued MCC, looking crestfallen. 'You could make a nice profit.'

'But we don't *have* it!'

'Going for a second time at seven hundred,' said the auctioneer.

'Don't you worry your head about that,' said MCC.

'*Sold to Povey's Antiquary!*'

'*Oh!*' howled Mrs Povey. 'Go and tell him we haven't got the money! Tell him it's a mistake! He'll have to auction the table again. I'll never be able to show my face here after this.'

'Now, now,' said MCC. 'Leave this to me,' and he jumped and squeezed his way round and over the chairs to the front of the hall, grinning to left and right at the munching, smoke-breathing dealers. He approached the table as if he were about to plunge into the shiny depths of its reflections, and ran his hands over its legs as a horse dealer might over the fetlocks of a thoroughbred mare. 'I'm sure! I'm almost certain . . . it must be . . . it's so much like . . . it's been a long time since I saw it, of course, but I'm sure . . .'

The dealers pricked up their ears like a pack of wolfhounds, and for all the auctioneer coughed and said, 'Shall we get on?' and the porters came to carry the table away, MCC would not allow it to be removed from the stage.

'Gentlemen! Gentlemen!' he cried, turning on his audience. 'I'm glad you're here today to share in my good fortune. I do believe . . . though there's no way of knowing for sure . . . but this table is so much like the one in the poem!'

'What poem?' The murmur ran round the hall.

'What poem? Oh you must know it, surely! *The Night the Prince of Wales came Late to Dine*.'

'The Prince of Wales!' murmured the dealers, for the mere mention of royalty rings like money in the ears of an antique dealer. And then, because they did not want to look ignorant, they began to nod nonchalantly to one another. 'Oh yes! By the Poet Laureate, wasn't it?'

'I thought Robert Browning.'

'No – Kipling – I'm sure it's Kipling.'

'Or Goldsworthy?'

MCC had somehow edged the auctioneer off his rostrum and now bent his face towards the microphone. His eyes were as large, dark and oval as the table itself, and filled with the reflections of his restless, munching audience.

* * *

The visit of His Royal Highness The Prince of Wales to the home of The Right Honourable Lady Bowdley, Hampshire, 1899.

First came the linen, like a fall of snow –
A level glacier, glazed by starch and heat,
Falling in sheer, white bluffs to the rug below
To fold across the eight, carved, lion-claw feet;

And then the candelabra – silver trees
Like those which, dragon-guarded, bore the fruit
Which Herakles fetched from the Hesperides –
All along the table, six took root.

No armoury of serried pike and sword
Ever displayed so many prongs and blades
As the cutlery laid out to grace the board
Of Edward, Prince of Wales, by the maids.

Beside the window Lady Bowdley stood,
Her fingers clasped, her noble face dismayed:

Would the Prince be late? And if he would,
Could the quail omelettes be delayed?

The guests trooped in, the cream of English stock:
The County Squire, the Marchioness, the Dean,
The Lady Swann in long organza frock,
The Judge, a second cousin of the Queen.

They stood and eyed the empty, gilded plates,
The empty glasses, bowls, tureens and cups,
And pondered, if the Prince of Wales were late,
When the Lady Bowdley would serve up.

The Breton chef waved temperamental hands
And wept into the simmering serving pans:
'Monsieur le Prince is ruining my flans!
I cannot answer for my baked meringues!'

The rumblings of the guests grew menacing,
Like distant thunder rolling round the sky.
There was a flicking out and tucking in
Of napkins into bodices and ties.

The Dean began to nibble on a roll,
The Lady Fortescue began to bleat,
'I think the Prince would want us, on the whole,
Not to wait all night but just to eat!'

So Lady Bowdley summoned up the soup,
The antipasto, whitebait, langoustine, the
Avocados, prawns and cantaloup,
The pâté, lamb and pestoed tortellini.

Fish course began with lobster thermidor,
Then plaice and halibut and Dover dab,
And shark steak, roll-mop herring and yet more
Unidentifiable bits of crab.

Then came water-ices – lemon sorbet –
A frothy frost of egg white, slightly sweet,
To clean away the taste of fish before they
Plunged like porpoises upon the meat.

The Lady Edgar eased undone her zip
And drove her fork into the Vicar's hand
As they contended for the dish of chips.
The Duchess said, 'These artichokes are *canned*!'

Beef bled like a casualty of war.
The pork was pale as snow, with golden rind.
The more the guests devoured, it seemed, the more
The smoky stoves disgorged of other kinds.

The lamb was studded with a hundred cloves
Of garlic, plumed with fronds of rosemary;
The partridge, quail and widgeon sat in groves
Of feathers or on nest of vermicelli.

To sounds of silver trumpets in they bore
A roast swan stuffed with pineapple and dates.
The Bishop loosed his tie and softly swore,
And sped to clear his overloaded plates.

The wine poured down like Iguaçu Falls;
It dyed the Squire's beard a bloody red;
And champagne splashed the oaken panelled walls,
And corks lodged in the ceiling overhead.

Glazed ribs and cutlets dipped in creamy sauce,
Slivers of veal and ducklings on a spit:
No sooner had they gobbled up one course
Than dozens more delights succeeded it.

Hastily the Judge took off his coat
And belt and rolled his sleeves up and began
To bawl, demented, 'Pass the gravy boat!'
And carve great slices from the honeyed ham.

Like Death Valley where the sun-bleached bones
Of buffalo litter the burning ground,
The greasy table sways and rocks and groans
Beneath stripped carcases heaped up in mounds.

But though the muscles of their jaws were flagging,
The greed of man and maid alike was not.

The Marchioness was shrilly heard a-bragging
That *she*'d like second helpings of the lot.

'Oh save a little appetite for sweet,
My lords and ladies, gentlemen and friends!'
The Lady Bowdley sweetly did entreat,
As if so mean a meal called for amends.

There was a rending then of dinner suits,
Of shirts and blouses, frocks and cummerbunds,
As trolleys brought in gateaux, tarts and fruits
And *crêmes brûlées*, compotes and sugar buns.

Dark-backed éclairs and trifles, cherry flans,
And Baked Alaska, *bombe surprise* and tubs
Of caramel, and rum babas, and pans
Of flaming *crêpes Suzettes* and syllabubs.

'Bring in the port, the brandy, the cointreau!
The *petits fours*, the after-dinner sweets!'
Called Lady Bowdley from some spot below
The table, in among a host of feet.

Holding his sides, the Squire sprawled and gasped
Face down among the lemon meringue pie.
The groaning, grinning, gurgling Bishop clasped
An empty brandy glass against his eye:

'I see no chips!' he chortled, then expired –
Likewise the Marchioness, so grossly fat.
With sugar-spangled hair and cheeks affired,
They slithered from their chairs on to the mat.

The Prince of Wales drove up with honking horn,
But no reception waited at the door.
The stubs of candles glimmering forlorn
Showed the sad story written on the floor.

Amid the pools of candlewax and wine,
The county's gentry and nobility
In ragged finery all lay in line –
Victims of too much hospitality.

* * *

The floor of the hall was littered with half-eaten sandwiches and paper bags. A dozen dealers were scribbling notes on the back of business cards and, as MCC Berkshire stepped from the rostrum and strode back down the hall, they pressed their messages into his hand or into the pockets of the green corduroy jacket. He resumed his seat and read all the notes through, showing now one, now another, to Mrs Povey. At the sight of each one she would give a little hysterical shriek of laughter and begin sobbing again. After a few minutes he leaned across the chairs in front and said to a man in a black wool coat with an astrakhan collar, 'I hate to part with the table, but my employer Mrs Povey instructs me to accept your offer of one thousand pounds.'

The man in the astrakhan collar paid cash, and MCC was able to give seventy clean ten-pound notes to the auctioneer. 'Want a job, young man?' said the auctioneer with a wink. 'I can always use a good talker.'

'Thank you for the kind offer, but I'm very content with Mrs Povey,' said MCC, and Ailsa's mother burst into tears all over again.

After that, MCC took very little interest in the proceedings, but slipped a small book out of his pocket and read, wholly and completely absorbed, while the auctioneer's patter rained down on the assembly. Ailsa glanced over MCC's shoulder. It was poetry he was reading, of course.

CHAPTER SIX

THE HARPSICHORD: A STORY OF HONOUR AND TRUST

Then they came to cut off the telephone.

Mrs Povey thrust money at the engineer but he only sniffed and said, 'Shoulda paid it biffor, Mrs. It'll cost a packet for you to be reconnected now. Yer on a party line or they could just of cut you off at the Exchange. But yer on a party line, see, so here I am to cut you off.'

Ailsa was reminded of the nursery rhyme:

Here comes the candle to light you to bed,

And here comes . . . the Post Office engineer to cut off your phone.

Mrs Povey went upstairs to have a cry, because of the shame of being cut off.

He was a big, brawny man, the engineer, with tattoos on his forearms. He had short, thin hair, and a face so weather-beaten that the lines and creases showed white like the loose cottons on a teddy bear. He walked with a decided roll, to and from his van, to fetch the dreadful instruments of Disconnection. At the sight of MCC lying along the *chaise longue*, reading, he bared a few tobacco-stained teeth and muttered, 'Idle, good-fer-nuffing pansies.'

MCC looked at him coldly over the edge of *Plunder of the Spanish Main!* and asked, 'Is it my fault if there's no work on the ships any more?'

The sneer disappeared so fast from the engineer's face that it might have short-circuited. 'Don't I know it?' he groaned. 'What, Merchant Navy, are you?'

'Not now,' said MCC dolefully, just as though last week he had been.

'Which ships? What line? Where? I was on the *Avro* – beautiful little lady she was, biffor she got herself sold to Sri Lanka. Went for scrap last year. Tragic. Tragic,' moaned the engineer. 'These days it's all supertankers and no-one needed to crew them. It's curtains fer the likes of us. Got a fag?'

MCC cemented the friendship by fetching out a battered pack of Senior Service cigarettes from his jacket pocket (though Ailsa had never ever seen him smoke). It was as if the anchor on the packet cleaved the two men's hearts together. 'Tragic. Tragic,' said MCC lugubriously. 'Of course the *real* ships were the sailing ships. Wish I'd been a naval man then. Concertinas on the poop deck. Shanties on the fore bits – and the songs circling up to the crow's-nest like seagulls on the wing!'

The engineer's eyes drifted involuntarily towards the ceiling, and his lips smiled. 'Got a Yamaha electronic organ misself,' he said.

This seemed to come as no surprise to MCC. But perhaps he had already seen the roll of sheet music protruding from the pocket of the blue overalls.

Ailsa, watching through the kitchen door, pushed aside her homework and hurried into the shop. She dragged the winged armchair up behind the telephone engineer, then curled up herself in a basket chair alongside him. The engineer was put out – irritated that his conversation had been interrupted. 'What d'you want?' he said rudely.

Ailsa waved him into the chair. 'Sit down and listen. MCC's going to tell you a story. There's no point arguing. He'll tell it anyway. You may as well give in.'

Unease, suspicion, curiosity and eagerness, all at one time, shared the weather-beaten face between them. He sat down, but took the doomed telephone on to his lap, as if to say that no last minute rescue bid would save it from grisly execution. 'Get on wiffit, then.'

* * *

'Look what we found, Captain!'

They dragged the little boy out from behind a barrel in the hold, and held him up by his collar and belt. 'A stowaway, Captain!'

'Fetch him up. Let me have a look at him!'

A sailor ran up the ladder with the stowaway over his shoulder, and set him down, blinking and dazzled, at the Captain's feet. 'Up brat! Up!' snarled the Captain, examining the trembling heap with the toe of his boot. 'Name? You do have a name, I suppose?'

'Ned, sir,' said the stowaway. 'Ned Cox, sir. And I didn't mean no harm, sir, honest!'

The Captain's top lip drew back off a straggle of small, pointed teeth. 'Not mean harm, sir? Stow away and not mean harm, sir? Ride without paying your passage? Help yourself to victuals every mealtime, I daresay? Smuggle yourself aboard to save capture for your crimes, I daresay?'

'Oh no, sir! I never did no crimes, sir, honest!'

'Honest? But honest is what you are not, sir. And do you know what I do with dishonest little stowaways? I throw them over the side, sir, to feed the sharks on the way down and the crawling things on the bottom. Do it, Second.'

Nobody moved. Beyond the Captain's shoulder, Ned could see the green horizon slanting first one way then the other as the ship rolled. The hands on his clothing tightened, but still nobody moved. In the distance he could hear somebody crying, and did not realize that it was himself. In the distance, too, a voice said, 'You don't mean it, Captain.'

'Mean it? Of course I mean it! Do it, then perhaps we can all get back to work.'

'You could put him in the brig, sir, and put him off in the Barbadies, sir . . .'

'If you bandy words with me, sir, it's the brig for you and the sea for him. You do it, bo'sun, if the Second takes a dislike to my orders!'

The hands on Ned's shoulders changed, but still nobody moved a step closer to the rail.

'I couldn't do that, sir. It wouldn't be right.'

'Right? I'll tell you what's right. On board this ship what I say is right and what you think ain't worth a ladle of tar. Right?'

'*Thou shalt not kill.* I couldn't go against my Christian conscience, sir.' An unhappy murmur of approval ran through the assembled crew, and the sailors who had found Ned and handed him over, murmured loudest of all, and their fists were clenched in their gabardine trousers.

The Captain stepped forward and snatched hold of Ned by the wrists and pulled him so sharply towards the rail that the ragged back of his shirt was left in the grip of the bo'sun. He swung the boy bodily over the side, like the whip-end of a rope, but kept hold of his wrists. Beneath Ned the sea glittered and made mouths – deeper and deeper gullets of dark green water. His feet banged against the planks of the ship and his arms were half out of their sockets.

'It's not right, Captain,' said the bo'sun loudly, and the muttering grew to a hubbub, and the whole length of the rail was hidden by sailors leaning over.

'You mutinous pack of blubbering women,' said the Captain contemptuously. 'If you want him that much, you fish him out like the herring he is.' And he dropped Ned into a shattering world of sharp-flying emeralds, rib-creasing cold and salt-tasting panic of bubbles as the water rushed up over his head. Surfacing was like running up an immensely long staircase with no treads.

At once a tail-end of heavy ship's rope hit the water beside his head and he made a clumsy grab at it and it slipped through his hands. His head went under again.

'Catch hold boy, quick!' shouted a dozen voices from overhead, and the rope came down again, just out of reach. Ned could see the side of the ship slipping by him at great speed, like the barnacled flank of a massive whale.

The stern was coming closer, and once the ship had passed him by, it would not turn back. A third time the rope hit the water, and he grabbed tight hold with hands and feet and teeth and knees and was hauled up the splintery side of the speeding square-rigger.

A dozen pairs of hands pulled him over the rail, but they dropped him on the deck, and the first face he saw was again the Captain's, pushed close against his. 'Well, get to the crow's-nest, boy, and keep watch for a day. I reckon you'll be sorry these jellified women here fished you out. I'm putting you off at Barbado.'

He stalked to his cabin, and the sailors who had defied him turned their eyes away from Ned as though he were a sin they had rather not have committed. Everyone would suffer for crossing Captain Lock.

'Better do as he says, lad,' said the bo'sun. 'Have you ever climbed rigging?' Ned shook his head. 'Well here's your chance to learn. Take a can of water with you and keep a sharp look-out. If you see a ship, sing out. He'll maybe soften before Barbado if he thinks you'll make a ship's boy.'

The mast rose out of the deck like some naked, lopped, jungle tree shrouded in vines of rigging. The slack ropes sagged beneath him so that he was like a small animal struggling in a net, a fly trapped in a spider's web. He looked up at the crow's-nest and the white midday sun was behind it, so that his eyes were momentarily blinded. By the time he reached the first yard-arm, the joints of his arms and legs were burningly useless and he thought he would simply cling there until he fell. But when he looked down, the deck below seemed to be racing from side to side as the ship rolled. It was a sight so unnerving that he kept climbing despite himself, with sweaty hands on the coarse rope, up among the huge, flapping sails.

The crow's-nest was a miserable little basket, no bigger than a bath-tub. As the ship rolled, it swung way out to port side, then to starboard side. Even a hardened sailor gets sick in the crow's-nest. Ned felt certain he would die with each flick of the masthead. The sun dried the sea salt on his clothes and on his skin until he was caked in corrosive white, and burning, burning. There was nothing to do but crouch down in the bottom of the basket and cover his head with his salty arms and groan.

They left him there all night, when the stars and their reflections in the sea became indistinguishable and both were flecks of ice which pierced him through and through, as the mast tossed him across the whole arc of space, to and fro. As for keeping watch, he would sooner have been born without eyes than scan the lurching horizon.

He never so much as saw the pinnace coming. It closed out of a heavy sea mist in the morning, and the first he knew of it was the cry of 'Pirates!' from the deck.

Captain Lock, who had been drinking heavily and whose cruelties of the day before were nothing but a forgotten blur, demanded to know who was in the crow's-nest, who had failed to keep watch. But it was too late for blame. The pinnace was upon them, closing from astern as if she would gouge the side out of them with her bowsprit. From point-blank range she fired her cannon – first at the yards, so that tackle and ropes rattled down like twigs through a stormy tree – then deeper and deeper into the body of the ship, but above the water-line. As the bo'sun ran out one cannon, it crashed through the weakened deck into the hold below. Another rolled clean through the shattered gunwale and plunged into the sea. There was utter confusion among the sailors – whether to fight or whether to surrender. At their backs stood Captain Lock, cursing them, blaming them, threatening them with a hangman's noose if they allowed his ship to fall to pirates.

There was only one musket-shot. It came from the yard-arm of the pirate ship and silenced the Captain in the space of a single curse. He fell rigidly, toppling over the side just before the two ships grazed together with a flurry of sparks from the iron bolts clashing. A final cannon blast shattered the mast high up and it fell, like the top smashed out of a tree by lightning, into the outstretched yard-arms of the pinnace. The two crow's-nests rubbed cheeks.

Ned was dislodged from his nest, and tumbled into the upper rigging, unseen. The sailors of the merchantman gave him no thought: they were busy surrendering themselves and their cargo to the pirates.

The shouts of the boarders were blood-curdling, but they had no apparent interest in blood-letting, now that Lock was silent. Having emptied the Captain's cabin, they locked the crew inside it and fell like locusts on the contents of the hold, transferring them to their own ship with the skill of long practice. Then, with a rattle of small-arms fire, they sheered away. The rigging snagged in the pinnace's topmast, and pulled the pillaged ship over to starboard before the ropes snapped and broke free and left the merchantman wallowing side-on to the swell.

It was in no great danger of sinking.

Ned found himself head-down in a sort of hammock of rigging, sliding and falling and yelling his way towards the deck to the amusement of the deckhands below. They caught him in strong, rope-calloused hands, and carried him along like a ritual sacrifice, and set him down in a terrified bundle at the feet of their own Captain. 'Look what fell out of the yards, Skipper!'

Ned's eyes travelled up from the sagging, shineless boots to the cracked leather belt, the sabre and pistol and axe, and the musket held pinned under one threadbare elbow. The pirate skipper's face was turned up towards the masthead, assessing the damage done by the tumbling crow's-nest. He was very tall and lean, with creases in his face as deep as sabre cuts, and eyes shut down to slits with looking into the sun. He had a three-day growth of black beard and a pony-tail of raggedly cut hair. At last he looked down at Ned and scowled. 'Not hurt, then?' he said. 'Sorry about your skipper.'

'He wasn't mine. I was stowed away, sir.'

'Ah.'

'Please don't kill me, sir.'

'Excuse me?' The pirate captain put his hand behind one ear. 'It's the noise of the cannon. It always leaves me a little deaf. It passes, though. Come to my cabin. You must be knocked about. You can lie down there.' He had an unsmiling, melancholy face, as if preoccupied with some distant sadness. In his cabin he poured himself a jug of wine from a cask and his hands shook and the pewter clattered against the barrel.

The entire cabin was strewn with books and charts, and there was a musical instrument – a spinet – in one corner, anchored by twine to nails in the wall to save it crashing about in rough weather.

'Why did you stow away, boy?' he said. 'Speak up, if you please. Remember my poor distressed ears.'

'Me ma died and me pa drank,' said Ned.

'Ah.'

'I thought to go to the New World and be a trapper. But they found me. And the Captain dropped me over the side and the men pulled me out and then the captain sent me up to the crow's-nest all night. And then you . . . and then I . . .'

The pirate skipper banged his ear irritably with the heel of his hand. 'Something of a tyrant, that captain, by the look of him. You come to know after a time. There are those who can rally a crew and there are those who can only bully them. Yours was one of the bullies. I could see that from a furlong off. It's easy to pirate from a bully: the crew's half on my side from the start. There's mutiny in their hearts already. That's what I tell myself when I shoot a bullying ship's master. Maybe I saved his crew from mutiny and ending up like me and these other poor creatures. That's what I tell my conscience.'

Ned nodded, but he was not following. All he could think to say was, 'You're English.'

'No. No, boy. I *used* to be English. Now I'm a citizen of the sea. There! I told you my ears would come back to me. I heard you well enough that time. Yes. I was English once – a lifetime or so ago. I was First Officer on a big wooden-wall out of Gravesend. The master was of the bullying breed. A flogger. A stopper of rations. A keelhauler. The men mutinied. I took their side. And that was the end of us. Mutiny's easy. It's afterwards that's hard.' He was staring out of the leaded bow window that flooded the room with light. 'That wooden-wall was too slow for piracy. I changed it for this.' There was a chink of music, and he turned round and saw that the boy was standing at the spinet, his hands frozen guiltily over the keys.

'I'm sorry! I didn't mean to touch it!' cried Ned.

'That's all right, lad. Do ease up. You've heard too many stories about pirates. It's overfired your imagination. Do you play the spinet, then?'

'Me pa's a bricklayer,' said Ned with a snort, but Captain Broome did not seem to hear.

'It's very out of tune now, I fear. One thing to pirate a spinet. It's another to pirate a spinet-tuner. It's a woman's instrument, of course. Oh for a shipload of harpsichords to loot!' He crossed to the keyboard and began to play. He had to stand with one knee and his shoulders bent, for indeed the spinet was built for a woman to stand at and not a tall man. But as Ned watched him play, he could suddenly see past the stubble of beard and the ragged hair, the sunburn and the dishevelled clothing, the axe and pistol and sword-belt. He could see precisely how this man had looked when, in high-collared tailcoat and breeches and with a neatly combed queue of hair tied in a black ribbon, he had stood in some drawing room and entertained the ladies to the music of Telemann and Bach. The music was the sweetest noise Ned had ever heard, for it spoke aloud that he was in the hands of a gentleman – a fact which dried up the hungry ocean, melted the sword's edge. He had never heard a spinet played in all his life, but every note spelled out safety. He sat down on the pirate's bunk and fell asleep leaning against the bulkhead. Captain Broome went on playing.

A week later, a stray cannon-ball, fired from the afterdeck of a fleeing clipper, crashed through the wall of Broome's cabin and smashed the spinet to atomies. It served no purpose, for the clipper was caught and boarded and lightened of her cargo of sandalwood in the space of two hours. The pirates cut down her mainsail and left her wallowing while they made good their escape. It was only after the pinnace was over the horizon, that the battered crew of the clipper noticed the rowing boat cast adrift by the pirates.

In the bottom of it lay a boy roped hand and foot, and a canvas holdall of the kind sailors make themselves out of sail bits. The ship's captain had the boat brought aboard, but he had little time for sympathy. 'Where were they bound? Where do they put ashore? Where will he dock to make repairs?' he demanded of the ragged little boy.

Ned shook his head and shrugged, and hugged the sailcloth bag to his chest. 'They kept me prisoner below decks, sir. I never saw nothing. They never touched land while I was aboard.'

'And how did they come to get you?'

'Fell out of the rigging when they rammed me ship, sir. Fell into their yards, sir. Then they were on me in a pack. Scared me witless, sir. Me heart's still jumping, sir. Permission to take some water, sir? They wouldn't give me no food nor water 'cepting what the rats wouldn't touch.'

'What's in the bag?'

'Nothing, sir. I was a-sewing it in the crow's-nest when they rammed us.'

But the Captain tugged it out of Ned's arms and cursed as he pricked his hand on a needle embedded in the seam. It was not unheard-of for pirates to put a man aboard a ship to slit the captain's throat on a dark night . . .But there were no weapons hidden in the bag. There was nothing in it at all. In fact, it was only half made. He shoved it back into the boy's grasp and sent him below to eat.

At Tilbury a month later, Ned went ashore with the ship's cook who had a mother near the docks with a soft spot for motherless boys. She fed him on tripe and gravy and washed him in a tin bath and made him up a bed beside the kitchen range.

'Tomorrow we'll find you a ship in need of a cabin-boy, eh?' said the cook, 'or maybe you can come along o' me and be a pot-boy for me on my next ship?'

'Thanking you kindly, but I've got a thing or two to do afore I sail again.'

'Right-o. Reckon you can find yer way back here, after?'

'Reckon.'

'Ma'll have a plate a-waiting then.'

Next morning, with his half-made bag slung over his shoulder, Ned walked out of dockland and all the way to the glittering sprawl of London's West End. But while he was still in sight of the muddy river, he crouched down in the angle of a wall and, using his fingers and teeth and the needle and brute tearing, he rended the sailcloth bag to pieces. As each gold coin fell out of the double-folded seams and spun on the pavement, he clapped a hand or a foot over it to keep it from rolling into the gutter.

Far away, where flies reeled drunkenly in the heady perfume of the bougainvillaea, and the palm leaves overhead menaced the beach with sabres of dark shadow, and each dazzling wave unfurled lazily and in silence, a coin fell with hardly a sound on the flour-soft, flower-white sand. Captain Broome leaned forward and picked it up. 'Heads I win. The boy will come good.'

His crew, who littered the beach with their sprawling, jeered and groaned. 'Nah! Never. That boy's tiptoed away to Ireland or South Afriki to live on jam and champ-pain,' said the bo'sun.

'It's the foolishest thing I ever heard.'

'Drink it up in gin like his father, he will,' said another.

'Your trouble is, Skipper, you think the world's stuffed full o' gentlemen,' said the quartermaster. 'And it ain't or we'd all be home now with our wives and children.'

This was a forbidden topic of conversation, and the crew rounded on the quartermaster and threw fistfuls of sand at him. 'Don't! He's right,' said Captain Broome. 'The man we took the ship from by mutiny – old Gryce – by rank and by birth he should have been a gentleman. He wasn't. That boy we picked up – he should by rights be a guttersnipe, but just maybe he ain't. The toss of a coin says he ain't, and if I choose to risk my gold on a bad bet it's mine to lose.'

The men fell silent. They did not dare say any more once their captain sank into one of his morose, despondent moods. He slumped against the coarse hide of a palm tree, and threw pebbles at the toes of his own boots. His face was dark and brooding.

A man's shape, half rubbed-out by the glare from the sea, came running along the beach. 'Crate from England for you, Skipper! New in from London! I had 'em put it in the tobacco warehouse till you fetch it!'

Captain Broome laid down the pebbles he was holding and examined his open hands, flexing the fingers and smiling and smiling. Then he jumped up at a sudden thought. 'The tobacco house! That's too dry. I must go and fetch it quick and get it aboard.'

The harpsichord, in its crate, was lovingly packed

with wadding. Its rosewood polish was unblemished. Its wires and the hooks which plucked at them under the shining lid were as silver as mercury. As Broome leaned over the open chest and uncovered the keyboard, it smiled up at him with ivory teeth. 'The world not stuffed with gentlemen?' he said to himself.

Then a hand dropped on his shoulder and the barrel of a musket jabbed him in the spine. 'You are John Broome, late of the ship *York Castle*, and I arrest you for the capital crime of mutiny!'

A handful of British soldiers from the nearby colonial fort had ranged themselves at Broome's back, the bayonets mounted on their ornate, foolish weapons. The pirate's face showed no change of expression. His hands remained spread on the silent keys of the harpsichord. 'Was it the boy?' he said.

'What's that?'

'I asked who sold me to you,' said Broome.

'Takes no rewards to catch your sort,' replied the officer in charge. 'It so happens that the captain of the vessel what shipped this object out here was a certain Captain Gryce – that's right – the selfsame man you and your pack of mutinous dogs robbed of his ship and cast adrift in an open boat. He saw an English name on the casing: he had his suspicions, so he broke it open. Seemingly you was known for your music loving – a real comical figure in the fleet, says Captain Gryce – the laughing stock of Gravesend, you and your harpsichord-playing . . .'

The pirate breathed out a deep, shuddering sigh of relief. 'All's well, Lieutenant. I'm content to go with you. It will be good to see England again. You have no idea how much I have missed her.'

Not a man of his crew was captured – only Broome himself. He was put aboard a naval frigate, bound for London and his trial. Captain Gryce came to satisfy himself that the treacherous mutineer was chained fast in the reechy, swilling brig, and went away smiling with the pleasure of revenge.

After Gryce had gone back to his own ship, and once they were on the open sea, the captain of the frigate came and leaned through the hatch and said, 'We have that harpsichord aboard that was your undoing, Broome.'

'I advise you to keep it out of the salt air, sir,' said the pirate.

Next day, the Captain came again and leaned through the hatch and said, 'I know Gryce. A real bastard. He's lost another ship to mutineers since yours, you know?'

'I didn't know that,' said Broome. 'Another pack of lost souls condemned to wander the world.'

Next day, the Captain came and leaned through the hatch and said, 'I'm awful partial to music myself, Broome. S'pose you wouldn't come . . .'

And so Broome was freed from the brig on his word of honour as a gentleman, and played Telemann and Bach on a harpsichord sent him all the way from London by Ned Cox using his bagful of pirate gold.

A storm hit them in Biscay, and ripped out the foresail like a wolf tearing out a deer's throat. They ran ahead of it for three days, into the English channel, scattering tackle and jetsam. But they were driven ashore on Chesil Beach. The wind died the moment it had broken the ship's back on that unforgiving heap of pebbles. Even the next high tide did not shift her, and she sat forlorn but upright while the crew struggled to safety.

No trace was ever found of the mutineer, John Broome. The brig was flooded early in the storm, and it was assumed that he had been drowned in his chains. A lot of the ship's cargo was brought ashore, including a harpsichord from the Captain's cabin, though careless handling meant that it was soaked and stood corroding in a custom-house for months. Finally, some tall, disreputable type, saying that he worked for the salvage company, claimed it and took it away in a horse-cart. A spring tide cleaned the ship off the Chesil Beach in the space of one night and left not a plank.

Ned Cox, meanwhile, had returned to the dockland home of the ship's cook and sailed as his pot-boy on a voyage to the East Indies. He was the wonder of the crew, for he had a whole two gold pieces to his name and he swore he had come by them honestly.

* * *

Ailsa thought for a moment that the telephone engineer had fallen asleep, as children do who are read to at night. The shop had grown dark while MCC spoke, and it was time to close. Suddenly the phone in the engineer's lap rang once, jarringly loud, and tumbled through his knees as he leapt up.

'Hello? Yes? What? Right. All right, then. *Right*, I said!' he yelled into the receiver and put it back.

Up on his feet now he reeled his sailor's roll through the furniture, brandishing his rolled organ music in one hand like a cosh. He would have passed for a press-ganger looking for sailors to press into service. 'Where is it? Is it here? What happened to it?'

MCC looked at Ailsa and would not answer.

'It's here. I know it. Saw it biffor. In't there no lights in here?'

MCC said nothing, and Ailsa returned his look as if to say, 'Well I shan't tell him any of your lies.'

Just then Mrs Povey came downstairs from having her cry. 'What is he looking for, please?' she asked icily. 'It's time to lock up.'

'A harpsichord. Yer've got one. I seen it when I came in. Turn on the light for gawd's sake,' pleaded the engineer.

'Yes, we've got a harpsichord,' said Mrs Povey in some surprise. 'It doesn't play, though, I'm afraid. It got wet or something. If it were any good, it would be in a real antique shop. We've had it for years.'

Ailsa and MCC looked at one another and shook their heads and sighed.

The room flooded with light, and the engineer – reaching out to feel his way in the dark – found his hands poised over the keyboard of a stained, splintery harpsichord, standing drunkenly on three uneven legs. He played a chord – an utterly silent chord. There was only a sound of rust plucking on rust, like a cat sharpening its claws on a bristle mat.

But inside his head, the music played as loud as a breaking wave, and a light illuminated his weather-worn features like the St Elmo's fire which sometimes hovers round the mast-top of ships at sea. 'I'll rebuild it!' he exclaimed. 'The wife'll skin me, but I'll do it! I will! And I'll teach the nipper. I'll teach the babby to play!' Ailsa had a sudden vision of the ex-sailor's living room, its walls hung with pictures of ships, its shelves filled with the souvenirs of distant voyages, and the Yamaha organ and the harpischord eyeing each other across three centuries and a toddler's litter of toys.

MCC took his money and helped him put the harpsichord in the Post Office van. It was now long past closing time.

'Is the telephone cut off, then?' asked Mrs Povey dismally, though Ailsa said, 'Shshsh, Mother!' and MCC tried to silence her with a wink.

The engineer looked at his watch where it nestled among the hairy tattoos of anchors and sea-snakes on his wrist. 'Ah well, it's past my knocking-off time,' he said. 'I'll have to come back and do it tomorrer. 'Less you tell me *on your honour* yer going to pay. I'd pay if I was you. Reconnection costs a packet.'

'I will! I will!' promised Mrs Povey, scurrying humbly out of the shop behind him. 'Mr Berkshire earned some money this morning so I'll pay first thing tomorrow. On my honour!'

'Excuse me, sir,' said Ailsa, 'but who was it on the telephone just now?'

The engineer slapped the side of his head. 'Almost forgot in the excitement. Some rude creep called Clive's coming to visit you this weekend. Lord! The wife'll kill me when she sees that harpsichord. Reckon I'll tell her it's a cabinet fer the video. Just till it's mended.'

CHAPTER SEVEN

THE UMBRELLA-STAND: A STORY OF TEMPER

'But we always put him off!' groaned Mrs Povey.

'Why? What's the matter with him?' asked MCC.

'Uncle Clive? He's so . . . so . . .' said Ailsa.

'Exactly,' said her mother. 'He's completely impossible, he's so very . . .'

'Ah, I see,' said MCC, and had to wait until the Friday to judge Uncle Clive for himself.

There was just no pleasing Mrs Povey's brother-in-law. He knew so much better than everyone else. Nobody, from the ticket inspector on the train to the Prime Minister in his newspaper was fit to hold down their job since he, Clive Povey, could have done it so much better. He had a great many hobbies, all of which he did exceedingly well, whether it was restoring the eggshells out of which he ate his morning egg, or compiling a scrapbook of newspaper cuttings about tax fiddlers and dole-queue millionaires. The scrapbook was his proof that the country had 'gone to the dogs', and to Uncle Clive every high street and bus was more full of dogs than the Battersea Dogs' Home. He detested litter, whether it was a discarded cigarette-end or a tramp sleeping on a park bench. The trouble with litter was that it sat still too long and therefore smacked of idleness. If there was one thing Uncle Clive detested (and there were a lot more than one) it was idleness. He himself overbrimmed with energy – brusque, bright, battering energy. He blazed a path through the world, and behind him the litter swirled, the trees wilted, the clouds sagged and dogs cowered in terror.

And, of course, people were nice to him because of it. Eager to keep him from losing his temper, people were always respectful and polite to him, so that his attitude paid off. In fact, he really believed that people found him lovable and bluff, 'refreshingly honest' and so forth.

He was disappointed in his brother for dying. He was bitterly disappointed in the feeble efforts of the widowed Mrs Povey to run Povey's Antiquary. Time and time again he told her to sell up – but would she listen? A typical woman. She never listened to sound advice. 'A woman's place is in the home,' he said, and sent her advertisements from lonely hearts' columns and marriage bureaux, which she screwed up.

Like little crabs balanced on a smooth, round rock, Ailsa and Mrs Povey clung to each other and waited for Uncle Clive's ocean of spleen to overwhelm them. Always, in the past, they had fended off his threatened visits with desperate excuses, but now here he was, standing in the doorway in his open-toed sandals, tartan socks, ferocious checked suit and alpine hat. 'What moron wrote that rubbish on the shop front about *books*?' he demanded furiously, in his thick, Lancastrian accent. The purple veins were already pulsing in his bull-like neck.

'Hello, Uncle,' said Ailsa.

'How lovely to see you, Clive,' said Mrs Povey.

'Delighted to meet you, Mr Povey,' said MCC, rising from the *chaise longue*.

'Who the hell are you?'

'This is Mr Berkshire, Clive,' said Mrs Povey. 'He's been working here for a while.'

'Eh? Working here? Employing staff now, are you? Win the pools, did you? Since when could you afford to pay staff, Audrey?'

'Mr Berkshire is very good with people . . .' began Mrs Povey.

'You mean he talked himself into a job! Audrey, you must be even sillier than . . .'

'. . . and I don't pay him any wages – although I'd like to, of course, if I could afford it.'

'Eh? What's that? No wages?' Uncle Clive bore down on MCC. 'What's your game then, lad? You may pull the wool over a silly woman's eyes, but you won't fool me. What's your game? What's your angle? What are you up to?'

'I like it here,' said MCC, simply and quietly.

'Well y'can pack your bags and go and like some other place, son, 'cos you're out! Got me? Out! Probably some kind of a sex maniac or p-sychiatric case. You're mad to have him under your roof, Audrey. You're mad. I always said it. I told Tom on the day he married you: "she'll be the ruin of you!" . . . Well what are you waiting for, lad? You've had your marching orders. 'Op it.'

MCC blinked his brown eyes slowly, dispassionately, and Ailsa thought, for a great many seconds, that the bell she could hear was inside her head – a battle alert signalling the outbreak of war.

But it was only a customer standing on the shop mat, her way barred by Uncle Clive's huge suitcase. The bell rang and rang and rang.

'If you would permit me, Mr Povey, I shall serve this customer before I go,' said MCC, with icy politeness.

It was a nun from the convent. 'I was wondering if you had such a thing as a coat-rack?' she said. MCC sprang at once to the side of a beautiful, dark, solid-wood stand with a central pillar thick as a tree, four branching coat-hooks big as reindeer antlers, and a bentwood cage at the bottom to hold walking sticks and umbrellas. 'Well actually, all we wanted was a little row of hooks – you know – to nail on the hall wall. But thank you anyway . . .' said the nun.

MCC looked aghast. 'But what about the drips, sister?'

'I beg your pardon. Did you say "drips"?'

'I did! What about the drips from the umbrellas if you hang them on pegs on the wall. The carpet! The rotten floorboards directly below! What a hazard to the structure of the building!'

'Ah, but just for coats . . .'

'*Here* for coats,' said MCC, swinging from the great looping curves of wood to show their sturdiness. 'And *here* for the umbrellas. Note the lead lining in the base, allowing the water to *evaporate* gradually.' (His whole body mimed the life cycle of a raindrop caught in the Victorian umbrella-stand.) 'Do you have no umbrellas at the convent?'

'Well . . . y-e-e-s . . . I suppose we do. We do have. A dozen or more in fact.'

'I thought so! I mean, I know it would have been better – much better – if the last owner of this stand had *never owned* an umbrella, but then it seems to me that a convent is one of the few places a stand like this would be *safe*, given its history.'

Ailsa closed her eyes and willed and willed and willed the nun to say (and she did):

'Why? Who was the last owner of the stand?'

It was all the excuse MCC Berkshire needed. Like a ferret in a laundrette's washing machine, he seized his opportunity.

* * *

Dafyd Tresillick wore an oilskin when it rained (and it rains a lot on the west coast of Wales). He wore an oilskin and a sou'wester, even though he was no longer a member of the lifeboat crew. The oilskin was so stiff that it stood up on its own account – a headless apparition haunting the corner of the shed. In light rain he wore only an oiled-wool aran pullover, which smelled of tarry sheep when it got warm but which would keep the rain off nicely so long as nobody washed it in detergent.

Tresillick did not believe in umbrellas. Some people don't believe in God; Tresillick didn't believe in umbrellas. In fact, he disbelieved with a pagan fervour. He did not own one. He would not be given one – not for birthdays or Christmas or to please his wife. He said that any man who used one was a pansy, and any woman a public pest.

There was nothing Tresillick liked so much as a good, healthy, drenching, torrential great downpour of rain. When it did not rain, his allotment suffered.

The summer of 'fifty-two was not wet. In fact, there was a drought and, to his dismay, Tresillick toiled under a blazing sun every day only to see his lettuces shrivel, his tomatoes wither, his bean canes break out in a sickly crop no bigger than caterpillars. When autumn came, it blustered the burned leaves off the apple tree and knocked down the pebbly apples, but hardly a drop of rain came in on the wind. It was as if the great western sea itself had dried up in the summer and there were no waves for the winds to sip up and spit out on parched, blighted little Pontieth.

So it was a happy man who looked out of his bedroom window to see the first cold wet downpour of autumn drenching his thirsty lawn. 'Time for the winter underwear, Gwen. Where did you stow it away?'

His wife blushed, put in a burst of activity tidying the bedclothes, then hurried out on to the landing saying, 'I threw it all out in spring. It was a sight, it was really.'

After a stunned pause, Tresillick called after her, 'Well, didn't you buy new?'

There was a guilty silence, and the footsteps on the stairs halted. Gwen Tresillick, who was a Methodist, decided she must tell the truth, and she crept back into the room. 'The shops've stopped keeping them, love. They don't sell your vests no more.'

'What are you talking about, woman? Don't sell vests? What do you mean, they *don't sell vests*?'

Gwen winced. She was well-acquainted with her husband's temper, which was vile. 'Ah, vests they got a-plenty, love, but not *your* kind. Not the long-down-to-the-knees kind. Nor long drawers. Nor woollen combinations even. I've tried all over. Shops say there's no call for them these days.'

Tresillick opened and shut his mouth several times before he was able to ask, 'What's wrong with the world these days? Eh? Answer me that! What's the country coming to?' He went on to say this many, many times during breakfast, and was only stopped from saying it by an advertisement in the national newspaper which caught his eye . . . It was for the Army & Navy Stores. He slapped the paper violently with the back of his hand. 'Now *they*'d have them. My life on it they would!'

'But they're in London, *cariad*,' said his wife, soothingly. 'Tell you what. I'll knit you a nice all-over set.'

'Rubbish, woman! I'll go up there and buy them, that's what I'll do!'

'Up to London?' whispered his wife. (Tresillick slapped the paper again triumphantly.) 'But you've never been out of Wales, Dafyd! Well you've never hardly been into Pontypridd but twice since the War!'

He was offended. 'Never been out of Wales? I'll have you know I was in London the summer before I married you. Filthy smoky place and no air to breathe hardly. But if that's where I have to go to get decent drawers, I've no fear of going there, and don't you think it!'

Gwen gnawed her lip. 'Supposing the Army-and-Navy *don't* have your drawers, Dafyd? Terrible advanced they are, up there in London Town.'

'Nothing advanced about not selling a pair of good drawers!' declared Tresillick, and his wife was silent, knowing it was pointless to argue. For some reason, a great darkness welled up in her at the thought of Tresillick going up to London.

Next morning it was still raining when Tresillick boarded the first train of the day bound for London, but not so hard that he wore his oilskin and sou'wester – only the oiled aran sweater. His bald head gleamed as the raindrops rolled in great curves across his scalp like tiny airliners flying over the North Pole.

The train was almost empty, but as it crossed England it gathered a harvest of travellers heading for the capital. By eight-thirty it was stopping at commuter stations to pick up regular daily passengers.

Foolishly, Tresillick went to the buffet for a sandwich, and when he got back his seat had been taken by a woman with a child on her lap. The train by now was heaving with wet, steaming people braying in strange, un-Welsh accents:

'Filthy day, what?'

'Oh absolutely. Filthy. What a bane.'

'Different from last week, eh?'

'Can't complain, I s'pose. Had a good one, didn't we?'

'Absolutely!'

'Can't complain.'

But complain they did, as though the rain were the cruellest blow since God sent the Flood down on Noah. Tresillick rested his forehead against the window and looked out at the Home Counties grizzling by. It wasn't even raining hard! – a tame, refined drizzle, it was, that left pretty, diagonal, silver streaks on the dirt-caked windows. It was a mystery to him.

They reached another station and he gazed out at the damp, jibbering commuters who pressed and jostled towards the doors. They wore creased, lightweight trousers and skimpy barathea jackets, and pointed the way they were going with unfastened, flapping, dripping umbrellas, just taken down.

'Umbrellas, pah!' thought Tresillick. 'If God had intended us to keep off the rain, he'd have given us shells like turtles or lids like dustbins!' The newcomers clambered in, and the crowd in the corridor heaved tighter together until people were packed closer than beans in a tin. On Tresillick's left, a girl in a New-Look dress with a very wide skirt full of petticoats took up twice the space she warranted. And she wore heels so high that now and then she had to rest one foot and lifted it sharply and jagged Tresillick in the shin. On his right, a man in a bowler hat and suit attempted to flap the rain off his umbrella and only succeeded in sending a chute of water into Tresillick's shoe. Then he pressed himself hard against the Welshman, snagging his suit buttons on Tresillick's aran pullover, and said with a friendly grin, 'Terrible weather, eh?'

Tresillick thought of his allotment, lifeless as a desert, the birds pecking on his shrivelled marrows for a morsel of wet. 'What's wrong with it?' he snarled into the face so very close to his.

The windows turned opaque with the steamy breath of a hundred travellers, and wept condensation. It got very hot indeed in the corridor. The oiled aran sweater heated up and loosed acrid, choking fumes reminiscent of a dead sheep. The commuter's nose gave an unmistakable twitch and his top lip curled. With a disdainful flick of the wrist, he threw up a newspaper between them. It chafed against Tresillick's wet aran and left it black with newsprint.

The train gave a lurch as it came to a halt in London's Paddington station, and the girl in the high-heeled shoes stumbled and trod on Tresillick's foot: spearing it with her heel.

He limped off the train, and felt suddenly like a drunk thrown out of a pub at closing time. For in place of every one suited commuter he could see two, three, four. In place of every one umbrella, a forest of umbrellas. A dozen trains were disgorging identical people, and each had three legs: left, right and umbrella. Tresillick stopped, in sheer panic, at the top of the escalator leading to the Underground. Hosts of men with umbrellas were gliding downwards like the damned trooping down to Hell on Judgement Day. He turned to run, but the crowd was all pressing in one direction. A woman with a suitcase barged him on to the sliding wooden escalator, and there was no escape.

The flood of people washed him into an Underground train, a beast he had never seen before, which writhed its way through the ground like a giant bloodworm and carried Tresillick where he had no wish to go. His eyes ran wildly along the advertisements until a picture of a businessman in suit and bowler hat jeered at him, brandishing an umbrella, telling him to 'drink Ovaltine every night'.

'I don't want to!' whimpered Tresillick.

The Underground train spat him out at Charing Cross. He climbed up towards the light, but he could not shake off the host of black-suited, three-legged demons who pressed themselves against him, behind and on both sides, with a horrible, indecent intimacy.

Then he was out in the fresh air and the rain. He turned his face towards Heaven and thanked God for the gentle, soothing, cooling drops that splashed across his nose and cheeks and bald, sweating head. He had no idea where he was, but at least he was out in the rainy air!

With a bang that made him cry out with fear, a woman opened a telescopic, automatic umbrella right beside him. 'A new invention!' she said, laughing as he staggered sideways. 'Marvellously handy, aren't they? Super!'

Around him, the black-suited hordes opened their umbrellas in front of their bodies, like the great round shields of Viking invaders. Tresillick was a Celt once more, a dark-eyed Celtic peasant. Twelve hundred years of history melted away at the sight of those black, domed shields with central spike. A rainy mist blotted out the buildings and left only the giant, primeval River Thames writhing beneath them as the Vikings swept on to Charing Cross Bridge.

There was a wind blowing down the river. It buffeted and pulled at the myriad umbrellas, and the men plunged their bowler-hatted heads deep inside their umbrellas and marched on, blindly. As Tresillick turned to ask directions, the commuter behind pulled his brolly hard down over his head to keep out of the rain. The point of a single spoke sank into the top of Tresillick's bald head and gouged a tramline in his tender skin.

The pain robbed him of his last remnant of self-control.

He let out a blood-curdling cry and reached up, in self-defence and fury, and took the body of the umbrella and crushed and rended it into a buckled knot of spokes and rags. He snatched the handle out of the owner's hand and beat the wreckage against the bridge parapet, over and over and over again.

'I say!' cried the owner, as the rain pattered for the very first time on his tender bowler hat. He went to the defence of his umbrella because, when he was dressed for the City, it was a part of him as much as a leg or an arm or a nose. He lashed out with his briefcase and knocked Tresillick back against the parapet.

They struggled, they panted, they punched and clinched and rolled, along the metal parapet. The bridge shook as a train trundled across its lattice-work of iron girders. Sleepy commuters looking out through steamy train windows saw the death struggle between Viking and Celt, but had passed by before they could make sense of what they saw. Hurrying commuters on the pedestrian walkways of the bridge skirted nervously round the fight and hurried on. Those who, at the sound of a cry, chanced to look back, saw nothing; nothing but the ugly parapet of the bridge and the swirling misty rain beyond. They shook their heads and thought, 'Must have been mistaken.' For who would plunge off Charing Cross Bridge into the icy Thames with a cry of 'UMBRELLAS!'?

At the inquest, nobody could explain why Dafyd Tresillick should have travelled all the way up from Wales to murder Godfrey Pocock. Pocock was such a mild-mannered man – a bachelor bank manager who had sat at the same desk, day in and day out, for thirty years. Was there a woman involved? Had they been secret partners in crime and fallen out? The newspapers and the police speculated, but nothing was ever decided.

Pocock's secretary sniffed tearfully as she visited the murdered man's house. A pang of sentimental pain gripped her heart when she saw the solid, noble umbrella-stand in the corner of the hall. When had she ever seen dear old Mr Pocock without his trusty brolly? She fingered the bentwood curves tenderly, then, briskly blowing her nose, she made an inventory of the house contents and instructed the dealer to sell everything and send the money to Pocock's brother in Australia.

* * *

The nun's purse was open alréady. 'Oh the poor man!' she cried.

'The innocent victim? Yes indeed,' said MCC dolefully.

'No, no! Poor Mr Tresillick! To be vexed with such a temper! Oh it's a terrible demon to some poor souls not blessed with a peaceful nature. How much is the stand? I'll take it if it's not too dear – all supposing you can deliver it for me. Then every time I see it, I'll be reminded of those two poor men and I can offer up a prayer for them in my heart.'

'You'd best ask Mr Povey the price,' said MCC

without a trace of rancour. 'He's the businessman among us.'

Uncle Clive gave a start, like a stagehand in a theatre who finds the spotlight suddenly shining on him. He made an apologetic grab for his hat and belatedly lifted it to the nun, then clasped it to his chest, moithered with embarrassment. 'No charge! No charge at all to a lady of your . . . calling. I'd be honoured if you'd accept it as a gift to the convent. I'll bring it round myself to you this afternoon. Think nothing of it. Please. Thank you. Yes indeed.'

The little nun, quite overwhelmed with gratitude, passed out through the door as he held it open for her. He bowed as she went by. 'Oh but that's a nasty scratch you have there, Mr Povey,' she said sympathetically, indicating the livid red scrape across the top of Uncle Clive's shining head.

Ailsa slipped her hand into MCC Berkshire's.

He squeezed it and said, 'I'd best be going now.'

'No,' she said. 'You're not to.' And when Uncle Clive returned from waving the nun off, Ailsa mustered all her courage and said, 'I don't want Mr Berkshire to go, Uncle. The shop's been much better since he came.'

Uncle Clive still had his hat clasped to his chest, and the other hand rested on the top of his bald head. He shot MCC a look very akin to fear, but avoided the eyes, dangerous and deep as the River Thames. Uncle Clive said in a small, uncertain voice, 'Oh. Well, lass. That puts a different light on it . . . I didn't know the child was fond of him, Audrey. Why didn't you tell me the lass was fond of him, Audrey? You'd best keep him for a bit. See how things go on.'

'Yes Clive, all right. If you say so,' said Mrs Povey. 'Bring your case up to your room, won't you?'

'Oh. Right-o . . . But I ought to warn you: I can't stop long. I'm a busy man, you know. Can't waste much time on social calls.'

'*What a pity*,' said Mrs Povey and Ailsa and MCC, all together.

That afternoon, Mrs Povey sorted MCC's book-shelves while he was out with Uncle Clive delivering the hat-stand.

'What are you doing up there, Mother?' said Ailsa. 'You know I don't like you climbing ladders and things.'

Mrs Povey braced herself against the rungs of the step-ladder and steadied with her chin all the romances and love stories she had collected up from the lower shelves. She pushed them one by one into the darkest recesses of the top shelf. Then looking down at her daughter's upturned face (which was really growing to be very pretty indeed) she said, 'Don't get too fond of Mr Berkshire, will you, dear?'

'Why? Because he lied to that nun? I don't think it was so dreadful in the circumstances . . .'

'No dear. Not because he lied to the nun. I've got quite used to MCC's lies. Just don't get too fond of him, that's all.'

'But why not, Mother?'

'Don't argue, Ailsa. There's a good girl.'

CHAPTER EIGHT

THE MIRROR: A STORY OF VANITY

Overnight, Uncle Clive brooded on his generosity to the nun, and the more time passed, the more he regretted it. He slapped down a ten-pound note in front of Mrs Povey at breakfast next morning, though it seemed to cause him physical pain to take his hand away from it. 'That's for the coat-stand, Audrey. I won't see you out of pocket.'

'Oh there's really no need, Clive. It was generous of you, and I just hope I'd have done the same thing in your place.'

'Daresay you would. You're daft enough. But there's to be no more of it. I've had a look at your accounts, and the place is a shambles. Tuppenny-ha'penny takings. You barely charge more than you pay for a thing! Where's your profit margin? It's no good, Audrey. It won't do. Get on or get out: that's my motto. Get on or get out.'

His sermon was interrupted by a rattling at the still-locked shop door, and Mrs Povey hurried to let in the first customer, although it was long before nine o'clock. She never turned away trade.

It was a young girl, dressed in the most fashionable, unseasonal clothes – a t-shirt dropping off one shoulder, a tight skirt tapering down to fungussy tights and flat black gym shoes. An encrustation of ugly diamanté jewellery covered her chest, and she wore sunglasses despite the gloom of the late March morning and the interior of the shop. Behind her, down the street, came her elderly parents, stumbling in their hurry to catch up.

Mrs Povey had already opened the door before she noticed MCC's cricket trousers and green jacket lying neatly across the end of the big brass bedstead and realized that Mr Berkshire was not yet up.

The girl swaggered into the shop past Mrs Povey and roamed about, peering at things through the dense black lenses. She rounded the giant wardrobe and was greeted by the sight of herself in the massive, gilt-framed mirror. As big as a shop window, it all but reached the ceiling, its old, speckled glass supported by ugly cavorting cherubs and badly carved swags of flowers. Grand and tasteless, it had stood in the shop for as long as Ailsa could remember, having its dull gold paint chipped by the more practical furniture which came and went from around it.

The girl stood, hands on hips, admiring her reflection. It took some time to dawn on her that behind her, in the brass-framed bed, a young man reclined on one elbow, reading a novel called *Silent Screaming*.

'It's my birthday,' she said majestically. He looked up and wished her well of it, then returned to his book. 'I can have anything I like,' she bragged. 'I think I'll have this.'

Her parents bustled into the shop, breathlessly apologetic for the early hour, and they searched out their daughter. The mother gave a short shriek at the sight of MCC but then, since the young man himself seemed quite undisturbed – as if it were the most common occurrence in the world to sleep in an antique shop – she quickly felt sheepish and silly. 'Now *that*'s not very practical is it, my dear?' she said indulgently to her daughter when she heard about the idea of buying the mirror.

'I want it. Buy it for me. You said I could choose.'

The girl's father offered an embarrassed smile to Mrs

Povey, Ailsa and Uncle Clive. 'Once she gets a thing into her head . . .' he began to say uneasily.

'I want it. It's my birthday, isn't it? It's only a paltry mirror. I could ask for something much more expensive.'

'Yes dear, but . . .'

'I can have it, then?'

'It's so big, Angela darling.'

'And so ugly,' her mother whispered, not liking to offend the shopkeeper.

'I think your mother's right, you know . . .' began Mrs Povey.

'Now Audrey, shut it,' snapped Uncle Clive. 'It's not for us to go poking in our oar.' (He knew a sure sale when he saw one.)

'Be sensible, Angela, sweetheart. You don't want an ugly great thing like that, now do you?' said the father brusquely, but his voice wavered and Ailsa could read in his grey, seamed face a thousand defeats at the hands of his spoilt daughter.

Angela clenched her fists and turned and beat on the foot of the big brass bed, so that the shop was filled with an eerie, hollow resonance, like tubular bells. 'You're cruel and mean and I want it!'

MCC turned over, propped his head on the other hand and went on reading, as if there were no-one but him in the shop. There was a sharp change in flesh colour where the suntan of his arm gave way to the white of his shoulders. He yawned silently. This threw Angela into paroxysms of vexation and, with one eye on the mirror to see the dramatic effect of her tantrum, she hurled herself across the foot of the bed and beat with her fists on the counterpane. MCC drew his legs up out of harm's way and went on reading. The shop resounded with sobbing and shrieking and accusations and reproaches. 'I want it! You never give me anything I really want! You're mean and despicable and I hate you and you've ruined my birthday!'

'What she needs is a good slap,' muttered Uncle Clive, but broke off at the sight of the father's wallet being pulled unwillingly out. 'It's up to folk how folk ruin their kids,' he thought, and went searching for a price ticket behind the gilt mirror. Audrey Povey was bound to have priced it too low.

At the sight of her father's wallet, Angela paused for breath. 'Well, maybe if her heart's set on it . . .' said the poor father, humiliated and broken in spirit.

At that moment, MCC finished his book and shut it with a snap which made everyone jump. 'Care to hear a background to the mirror?' he asked.

'Not now, lad,' said Uncle Clive, rather too hastily.

Angela's mother pursed her lips and eyes to keep back the tears of humiliation, and shook her head. She wanted only to get away as soon as possible.

'I don't see how it would help, MCC,' said Ailsa.

MCC shrugged his white shoulders and leaned forward to ease his crumpled clothing out from under the sprawling Angela.

'Well *I* want to hear it,' said the sulky girl, sitting up and adjusting her pout in the miror. 'Where does it come from? Whose was it?'

MCC sat back in bed, his hands behind his head. 'Let me tell you the story,' he said.

* * *

Eustacia Dare stood so close to the mirror that her breath made a cloudy patch which obliterated her reflection. She wiped it away impatiently.

'You're so beautiful, Eustacia! Marry me or my life is at an end. I shall join the Foreign Legion and hurl my body on to the bayonets of arab tribesmen!'

Eustacia fluttered her eyelids and smiled an enigmatic smile, trying to keep the corners of her mouth from lifting, so as to look like the Mona Lisa.

'You make a man mad with desire! You make life

sweet, but ah, too painful to bear! Won't you ease my aching heart and say that I may lay my life at your feet, sweetest child of loveliness?'

Eustacia risked a glance upwards through her lashes. Yes. Yes, it came off nicely. The rim of white which showed along the bottom lid added an air of doe-like fright to her eyes. If only her breath would not keep steaming up the glass.

'Oh but surely! The Lady Alice with her cloak of mink and gloves of turquoise expects to be your wife! She is a lady far more befitting your rank and station in life, my lord!' she whispered, and the girl reflected in the mirror looked oh so heartbreakingly demure and selfless.

'No, no! I was a fool ever to think I cared for her! It is you! It has always been you, Eustacia Dare! If you will not have me, no-one shall. I shall live a bachelor for as long as my disappointed heart shall beat! Oh spare me my life! Tell me at least that I may hope!'

'Poor man. Can I hurt you so terribly? My unschooled heart – oh yes, that was excellent, 'my unschooled heart' – cannot say whether or not I love you. Nay, perhaps only a kiss shall tell.'

'You mean . . .? Can you really mean . . .? Is it possible that an angel should stoop down from heaven to kiss this worthless lump of clay?'

'You may. In fact I desire it, Captain!'

Eustacia pursed her lips, closed her eyes and pressed her cheek and mouth in a lingering, rolling motion across the plate glass. Fortunate Captain – to taste a kiss bestowed by the fabulous Eustacia Dare. She thought perhaps he might be struck speechless at this point, and she stepped back from the mirror to admire the overall picture of herself in her party dress of white muslin.

'Eustacia! Where is that girl? The guests will be arriving!' A querulous voice climbed its way up through the rambling levels of the house and found her where she stood in her mother's bedroom, placing her button-booted feet this way and that to find out the best effect.

She picked up the picture hat off the old-fashioned four-poster bed and tied the gauzy sashes under her chin. No. No, it was better off the back of her head, resting on her shoulders, with the curve of the brim surrounding her head like a halo and the white gauze pulled tight across her elegant throat. It looked nonchalant that way – as if she had just run in from the garden, not expecting guests. She pinched her cheekbones to bring a look of flushed health to the soft, pale skin then, putting on her long, white gloves, she went downstairs for her garden party. It was Eustacia's birthday.

Coming from the dark house into the sunshine, she had to pause on the terrace and let her eyes adjust to the brightness. The guests were mostly arriving by foot – neighbours who found it just as pleasant on such a shiny day to walk across their lawns or across the park to reach the banker's house. They were not yet mingling, but stood about in family knots, like clots of cream waiting to dissolve into coffee: the Arbuthnots and their son, Harry; Aunt Maxine and Cousin Gloria; those frightfully common people who were something to do with her father's work; the widowed sisters and their appalling lodger, the Post Office clerk; various of Eustacia's schoolfriends with their older and younger brothers. Eustacia craned her head this way and that trying to see between and beyond them to something, to someone else.

But there was no-one else. There was no uniform, no grey morning suit, no knee-high boots such as Rochester wore in *Jane Eyre*, no exquisite profile gilded with a beard, no dark tumble of Byronic curls breaking over the collar of a hunting jacket. Eustacia's spirits sank. They were all people she knew, and those she did not know she felt that more than five minutes would be wasted on knowing them.

Her schoolfriends introduced their brothers. There was George-this and Gordon-that and Teddy Pickles and Henry Block. Not one was past seventeen. Only William Bingwall was taller than her and then only because his body was so thin and narrow that he must have been put through the mangle as a baby. So thought Eustacia, cursing her friends for bothering to have such insignificant brothers.

'Happy birthday, if I may say so!' It was the Post Office clerk. 'I thought you might . . .' He thrust a bunch of flowers into her hands.

'Oh. Yes,' she said, and she thought, 'What a paltry bunch of flowers. I don't even like chrysanthemums. Lord! I do hope it doesn't mean he's in love with me. How dare he have the effrontery to even . . .' But it did not seem as if the Post Office clerk were in love with Eustacia, because after shuffling his feet for a minute during which neither of them said anything, he shuffled away towards the refreshments and asked for a beer.

'Do meet my brother, Nigel,' said Mary.

'Glorious day, isn't it?' said Nigel, sticking out a hand for her to shake. 'Many happy returns, what!'

'His teeth stick out and his jacket sleeves are too short,' thought Eustacia, retrieving her hand as soon as possible. 'What an odious boy.'

She positively cut dead Teddy Pickles. For although, in five or six years, he might be reasonably well off and his face might not be too bad with a beard, Eustacia had long since written him off for having such a ridiculous name. 'Eustacia Pickles.' Ha! How could any man of sensitivity foist such a name on a wife? It showed up his parents for the peasants they were that they had not changed their family name to something more distinguished.

'May I say that you look stunning in that dress,' said a voice, and Eustacia turned, her hopes rising like a hot-air balloon.

'Oh, it's only you,' she snapped. 'Why didn't Mater and Pater ask anybody half decent to my party.' It was only dull, ordinary, spotty Harry Crabb.

'Oh come on now! Don't bear a grudge! Just 'cos I said your hair looked like nuts and bolts in ringlets – can't you take a joke in good part, old thing?'

This was less than she deserved on her birthday. Eustacia felt tearful. She had raised her hopes so high, and once again she had been let down. This was *not* to be the party at which she met and captivated the man of her dreams. There was no-one here worth even bothering with. Their ordinariness was an insult in itself. She would not even ask these . . . these *dogs* to her wedding. They would spoil its picturesqueness. Why had she gone to such trouble to make herself look beautiful for this *hoi polloi*, these spotty, gawky, weedy, pigeon-chested boys and their unimportant relations. How long must she wait for Love to serve her her just deserts?

'You're not very attentive to your guests, my dear,' said her mother. 'Perhaps the young ones would like to dance. Cousin Herbert has brought his violin. Country dancing might be charming.'

'Oh Mater! Country dancing! When are you going to realize: I'm *sixteen*! I ought to be dancing Viennese waltzes in ballrooms with officers and gentlemen by now, not cutting a caper like a rustic at a barn dance! How can a young woman be elegant thumping across the lawn with a lot of *children*. This is a horrid party. Everybody is horrid and dreary!'

Her mother watched her flounce away across the terrace and struggled against the rising suspicion that she had raised a daughter exceedingly pretty but not altogether agreeable.

Eustacia knew differently. She was dimly aware of being unpleasant and sulky. But Eustacia knew that as soon as a lover came along who was worthy of her, he would unveil the *true* Eustacia, the radiant, serene, bountiful and gracious Eustacia Dare. Her hidden store of wit would at last hold the world in raptures – 'We never knew Eustacia had such a sparkling tongue!' – her natural modesty would conquer all dislike. Oh yes, she would be as nice as pie to people *then* – even Teddy Pickles with his ridiculous name, and Harry Crabb with his spots.

If ever the faintest doubt crept across her mind, and she suspected, even for a moment, that she was truly just as ordinary as the guests at her birthday party, she could always resort to the great mirror in her mother's vast bedroom. The mirror (and a little imagination) would confirm that Eustacia Dare was destined to be adored.

Then he came.

He rented the house on the far side of the park for the summer – an author who wrote poetry and novels not to earn a living but to stave off the boredom of a wealthy existence. His name was de Courcy and he was thirty years old, with hair the colour of gunmetal and a beard tailored almost as immaculately as his coat. He rode a bay horse around the park every morning before breakfast, and there were rumours that women had died out of love for him.

No dying for Eustacia. The young man was invited to dinner by Mater, and had agreed to come. His goose was thoroughly cooked.

'Oh I shall entrance him!' she told the mirror as she dressed in her Spanish lace. 'I shall carry my head *so*, and let my shawl drop off my shoulder once or twice, so that he may admire my skin.' She practised this. 'I shall say, "Mr de Courcy, sir, I have read your novels with the closest interest, but I feel that they are a little lacking in *passion*. Pray, have you ever been in love yourself?" – Oh, I shall hypnotize him! Should I allow him to kiss me tonight? No, "not until we are better acquainted" I think, though I shall perhaps *brush* against him a little as we ladies retire after dinner. Oh I shall captivate him! And when he is invited to balls in London by lonely dowagers and by his broken-hearted, cast-off mistresses, he will take *me* and dance with *me* instead of them, until the dowagers and the mistresses die of envy and the orchestra simply swoons away with rapture! Let me see. What shall be our first dance? A waltz, naturally! so that whenever he hears a waltz in future, his arms will rise involuntarily at the memory of holding me in his embrace! "Eustacia, my life was empty before I found you! I thank my guardian angel that you came when you did and drew me back from the brink of despair! From henceforward all my poetry will be in praise of your eyes. Dance with me now to the music of my beating heart!"' And she stepped up to the gracious reflection of herself in the great, gilded mirror. All around her an arch of cupids blew triumphant horns.

The reflection, close to, looked pensive, thoughtful – very charming but perhaps a little too solemn. Her smile (when she chose to use it) was indeed Eustacia's trump card. Let's practise that. The reflection bared its pretty teeth, but it was a poor semblance of a smile. Eustacia tried again. 'Oh no! That will never do, Eustacia! That smile is downright menacing!' She raised her hands into the waltz position and pressed the flats of her palms to the cool glass of the mirror to savour that imagined moment of triumph. Her reflection, of course, stepped up to the selfsame imaginary dance. Eustacia closed her eyes.

She could almost hear the music, as though down a long corridor or through a wall. She could almost feel the coolness of the poet's cheek against hers; his lips against her mouth; his heart beating against hers; his hands enfolding hers – cold. Oh! – cold!

Opening her eyes was strangely upsetting, for although she knew she was feeling fear – acute fear – the reflection of her face (pressed so close that the eyelashes were brushing the glass) showed no expression of fright. It wore only that triumphant, dazzling smile of hers – that trump card, that winning stroke.

And there was no cloud of breath.

As she tried to pull away, the hands gripping hers closed tighter, pulling her bodily against the cold, hard glass, against the yielding, soft, water-cold reflection. It received her and pulled her through a miasma of silver, like a drowning person sucked face down into a weirpool. She had a sensation of the silver closing over her – more like mercury now than water – and of her assailant rolling her, as a crocodile rolls its prey, beneath its body and into some deep, lightless cleft before leaving go and rising to the surface once more. Her hands were empty. Her cheek was no longer pressed to its cold reflection. Her heartbeat no longer rebounded against her ribs. In fact, her heart did not seem to be beating at all. And she was cold, cold, cold, and without air to breathe. She opened her mouth to cry out, but it filled up with molten and transparent silence.

The bedroom appeared cloudy and dim and distant, as though she were seeing it through a dirty window. Her sash still lay on the bed, but there was no reaching it – no more chance of reaching it than a skater who, once fallen through the ice, sees it congeal and refreeze overhead, blotting out the sky . . .

'Where is that girl?' said Mrs Dare. 'I'm so sorry, Mr de Courcy. I can't think what's making Eustacia so late down to dinner.'

'Perhaps you should go up and fetch her, Molly,' said her husband. 'She's probably day-dreaming again.'

But Mrs Dare had got no further than the hall doorway before the girl appeared on the turning of the stair. 'Where have you been, Eustacia! Hobbs is waiting to serve dinner and Mr de Courcy is here.'

'I'm sorry,' she said, but nothing more. In fact she remained almost silent throughout dinner, only venturing to ask Mr de Courcy if he were happy in his rented house. Her mother resolved to ask later if Eustacia were feeling ill, for she did not seem quite her pert, haughty self. She *looked* well enough, however: her hair parted on the other side for a change was most fetching. 'Eustacia, dear, have you hurt your hand?'

'No, Mater.'

'It's just that you're holding your spoon in your left . . .'

'I beg your pardon, Mater. I didn't realize it was incorrect. I do hope Mr de Courcy will not think me uncouth.'

Mr de Courcy did not. Mr de Courcy found it a most agreeable change to get away from effusive, witty women who chafed themselves against him at the least opportunity and made eyes at him across their dinner plates. After dinner, he ventured to show the pretty, quiet Miss Dare his new volume of poetry, although he was rather disconcerted to see that she apparently read backwards, running her finger along the lines from right to left. As is the way of modest or timid girls, she kept her eyes lowered a good deal. Only once did he catch them out in watching him, and then he choked on his coffee. For it seemed that a reflection stood in her eyes . . . of himself, yes, though not in the setting of the drawing room where they now sat, but in a vast bedroom complete with old-fashioned four-poster bed. A fine sweat broke out on his forehead.

A week later, news of the elopement shook the neighbourhood harder than an earthquake. The rented house on the edge of the park stood empty. The mysterious, the glamorous Mr de Courcy had disappeared.

The banker's pretty daughter was gone, too. As her distracted parents said, over and over again, they would willingly have agreed to a marriage if only they had been asked. But no, Eustacia had simply expressed the desire to step across the park and return to Mr de Courcy his book of poetry. And by nightfall neither was to be found for all the searching in the world. The poet had not even stopped to pack his clothes or personal belongings.

Some said he had taken the girl to Italy (as was the wont of romantic poets in that particular decade). Others said that he had interests in South American gold and had taken ship to Buenos Aires. The only positive last sighting was at six p.m. that day, when Teddy Pickles had passed by the poet's house. Hearing the sound of waltz-time, he had looked up and seen de Courcy beyond the lighted window of an upstairs room, dancing with a young woman – 'Except they were dancing sort of inside out, if you get my meaning: her right hand and his left hand up here – so – as if she was leading.'

Mrs Dare became very nervy and despondent after her daughter's elopement. She slept badly and woke her husband up almost every night with talk of the same nightmare. Eustacia, she said, came knocking on the far side of the bedroom mirror, pressing her face against the glass until it was all pressed out of shape, and clawing at the glass and calling and calling, but in a voice that couldn't be heard. So Mr Dare sold the mirror – 'It was always an ugly, fussy great thing' – and after that the dreams stopped.

'I take comfort in one thing,' Mrs Dare told her husband.

'What's that, dear?'

'Well, I used to feel, when Eustacia was younger, I mean . . . well, I couldn't quite find it in me to *like* her as a mother ought. She could be such a very vain, superior child, always thinking herself too good for ordinary folk. But somehow in those last few days we had together – after the poet came to dinner, I mean – I didn't find any trouble in liking her. No trouble at all, in fact. Quite the opposite.'

* * *

Everyone had moved away from the mirror, as though the floorboards might crumble like earth beneath them and tumble them into the mirror's watery, speckled reflections to drown there.

Uncle Clive was the first to break the silence: 'Tosh!' he said. 'Tosh and bosh! Never heard such rubbish in all my life. That'll be one hundred pounds, sir.'

'I don't want it,' said a disembodied voice from the far side of the bed, and Angela's white face, blindfolded with the dark glasses, peeped into view, as blind and wiffling as a mole. 'I don't want it. I don't want the poxy mirror. Look at it! It's all speckled. It makes me look as if I've got spots.' (But she did not look into the mirror when she said it.)

'Oh that can be resilvered easily,' said Uncle Clive through clenched teeth. 'Call it ninety.'

'I've changed my mind,' said the girl, peering at him murderously.

Her father put away his wallet, and her mother sighed deeply. They tottered out of the shop, their daughter snarling and snapping between them like some Rottweiler guard dog they could not control. 'We bought it as a puppy,' said their apologetic, glancing faces as they passed by the shop window, 'and look what it grew up into.'

'Oh wonderful!' Uncle Clive exploded into his flat accent, blunt as a mallet. 'Well, you're fired, for a start. I never did like the look of you.'

'Now, now, Clive,' said Mrs Povey. 'I don't suppose they would have bought it, even without Mr Berkshire's story.'

'Oh no? Oh no?' Fury boiled like sulphur in Uncle Clive's eyes and his red ears strained to part company with his grazed and trembling head.

'Furniture ought to go where it's wanted,' said MCC, almost to himself and with a sad, resigned smile. 'And so should I.'

CHAPTER NINE

THE ROLL-TOP DESK: A QUESTION OF WHODUNNIT

Ailsa would have thrown a tantrum except that she knew from the story that MCC would not like it. She was furiously angry that he, of all people, should give in to Uncle Clive's miserable temper. She decided to show her disgust by saying nothing at all, snatching up the book currently lying open on the *chaise longue* and starting studiously to read it. To some it might have looked like sulking, but fortunately any such unkind thought was banished by the darting blue flash of a whirling lamp as a police car drew up outside the shop.

Three officers came in – only two of them in uniform. They made the door look as small as a cat flap, and they filled the shop like bears lurking in a telephone box, and everything they looked at they seemed to be memorizing. No 'Good morning'. No introductions.

'Gentlemen, Madam, we are led to believe you may be in receipt of stolen property. You won't mind if we look around, will you?'

Uncle Clive had walked backwards into the living room. Mrs Povey began to laugh shrilly and deny everything. Like lions selecting the tastiest Christian to eat, the constables closed in on the dark-eyed, black-haired man who emerged from the maze of furniture as though he had just finished dressing for cricket. 'And who might you be sir?'

'Me? Berkshire's the name. I work here. What seems to be the trouble?'

'And what's your home address? Can you produce some kind of identity, sir? A driving licence? Cheque-book? Pay-slip?'

'Library tickets!'

'Not quite what I had in mind, sir. Your home address, please?'

'Oh, here. I'm living here, just now.'

'And before that? Where are you from?'

'Reading.'

'Reading as in Berkshire, sir?' said the constable, correcting MCC's pronunciation. 'Whereabouts in Reading, sir?'

'Oh, around and about. Here and there.'

The constable's face gave a twitch of pleasure, and he exchanged a knowing look with his colleague, his pencil poised over his notebook like a lucky pin over a treasure map. Here was a sure-fire villain. 'Your FULL name, if you please, sir.'

Behind them, their plain-clothes inspector, prowling the shop with his hands clasped behind his short gabardine car coat, uttered a cry of triumph and fell on the glass display case balanced on the wash-stand. 'And how do you account for having this *salmon* in your possession?'

Unperturbed, MCC stepped between the constables and explained to the inspector about the car boot sale at the railway sidings and how he had gone there to buy stock for the shop. 'Oh yeah?' said the inspector with a contemptuous twist of the mouth. 'That's what they all say: "Picked it up at a jumble sale, Inspector. Can't remember when or where or who sold it to me."'

MCC was not dismayed. He took a deep breath and said, 'I purchased this row of books here, the bookcase they are in and that distinguished salmon from an X-registration red Cortina belonging to a stocky man with a Latvian accent and a large sticker in his back window saying **I ♥ Dobermanns**. These other books I purchased, along with a marquetry writing box (now sold), from a blue two-door converted van registered in Liverpool. The receipts are in the top right-hand drawer of that roll-top desk behind you – although the Latvian gentleman would only go as far as to write "Cash reseeved, Ta, Mickey Mouse" on the back of an envelope, which is why I took the precaution of writing his registration number on the envelope as well.'

The inspector sprang at the desk and rummaged feverishly in the drawer. He asked to use the telephone, and Mrs Povey said yes, of course, and wouldn't he like some tea; wouldn't everyone like some tea? So while the detective inspector checked on the Latvian gentleman's car registration number, his two constables perched themselves uneasily on a horsehair sofa and fumbled with their notebooks with one hand while trying to balance a cup of tea and ginger biscuits in the other. One remembered that he had been half-way through noting down MCC's name. He was about to ask for it again when MCC, slumped back in the basket chair with his outstretched legs crossed at the ankles, waved his teaspoon in the direction of the gaping desk and said, 'In fact you might be interested in the history of that roll-top. It was Exhibit Number One in a celebrated court case, you know. A murder.'

The police constables' teacups rattled on their saucers. Ailsa, who had not read one word of the book in her hand, glanced at its spine. It was called *The Case of the Bloodstained Blotter.*

* * *

'I shall have to ask – gentlemen, ladies – that nobody leaves the house,' said Detective Inspector Farrell. 'A murder has been committed and statements will have to be taken. Sergeant. Be so good as to take notes?'

'Yes sir.'

Out at sea, the tide was turning, a bitter sleet began to rattle against the windows of the remote Scottish farmhouse where they now sat. The high wind set the electricity wires swinging, straining at their insulators, and the lights in the house flickered. In the next room, Angus Costick had been found slumped over the closed lid of his roll-top writing desk, a paper-knife in his chest and an IOU clutched in his hand.

In the living room, Costick's houseguests sat aghast and silent. A middle-aged woman, her greying hair fastened in an untidy bun, sobbed quietly into a handkerchief and kept saying, 'Poor Angus. Poor dear Angus!'

'Calm yourself, Miss Pyke,' said the inspector. 'I'm sure we can clear this matter up in no time at all. After all, the drive was blocked by snow from Friday night until this morning and there were no tracks outside when the police were summoned. So no-one has either come to the house or left it since then. I think we may safely assume that someone in this room is the murderer.'

Miss Pyke gave a sort of a wail and burst into renewed sobbing. The others looked at each other with bulging, startled eyes full of mistrust: Neville Costick (the dead man's nephew) was a large, shabby man with a whisky glass forever in one hand; Enid Costick was the victim's daughter; Timothy Gribley (the dead man's secretary) was a dwarf and one-time circus performer, and Wembley Poole was a business partner of the murdered man. There was also Mrs Beattie the house-keeper, lurking in the background, nervously flicking a duster across the sideboard from time to time. Outside, the undertaker's van drove away with what remained of Mr Costick.

Inspector Farrell drew his sergeant aside and said, hardly moving his lips, 'I shall now retire to the scene of the crime and there interview each suspect in turn. I always find the scene of the crime makes a guilty man jumpy – easier to catch out, you know. Remember these things, Sergeant. You may be in criminal investigation one day.'

'Very good, sir.'

'I've got it ninety per cent sewn up. It's the nephew, and I'll show you for why.' He led the way through the broken office door and sat his sergeant down where the dead man had been sitting five minutes earlier. 'You see, Troughton, death was caused by an upward blow to the chest – clearly a blow struck by someone very tall standing behind the man and reaching over his head . . . so!'

'Yes sir,' said Sergeant Troughton, easing the point of the inspector's fountain pen away from his tie.

'And who answers that description?'

'Either Wembley Poole or Neville Costick, sir.'

'Exactly. And whose IOU was clutched in the dead man's hand showing a debt of one thousand pounds *due yesterday*?'

'Neville Costick's, sir.'

'There you are, then. He owed the old money-lender money – couldn't pay – and stabbed him instead.'

Sergeant Troughton licked one finger and tried to wipe the ink off his shirt-front. 'There is just the matter of the locked door, Inspector, sir. The office door was locked on the *inside*. The housekeeper had to ask Neville Costick to break it down before they could get in and find the body. And there are no windows in this room for a murderer to have made his getaway.'

'Hmm . . . Well, of course I'm keeping an open mind about this, Sergeant . . . The only person we can eliminate altogether is the secretary, Gribley. He's not tall enough to have reached Costick's chest even when they were facing each other. He certainly couldn't have reached over a seated man and stabbed him in the chest. Send him in first, Sergeant. I need someone trustworthy to tell me about the others – and about the dead man.'

'Very good, sir.'

Timothy Gribley was ushered in. He eyed the desk with an expression of bitter grief, and blew his nose on a large handkerchief. His head was on a level with the top drawer of the roll-top desk, but after he clambered on to a chair, with the ease of long practice, he faced Inspector Farrell, looking anxiously eager to help.

'What manner of man was your late employer, Mr Gribley?'

'Oh! A dear, kind, generous man, sir!' exclaimed Gribley. 'Firm but fair, I always call him . . . called him. I know there was some as didn't care for him, but I never had anything but kindness from him from the day I began work here. And generous with his wages, too, sir.'

'I see.' Inspector Farrell tapped on his teeth with the fountain pen. 'Who exactly did you mean when you said "some didn't care for him"?'

Gribley seemed embarrassed. 'I'm not one to tell tales. There's confidential secrets involved. I was a *confidential secretary*.'

'A murder has been committed here,' said the inspector sternly.

'In that case . . . I'm loath to say it . . . but you do know that Mr Costick's nephew Neville borrowed a large sum of money from Mr Costick only a year ago . . . and I don't think he's in a position to pay it back.' (Inspector Farrell gave his sergeant a knowing look.) 'And then Mrs Beattie the housekeeper was given notice last week for drinking her master's sherry and other pilfering around the house.' (The sergeant's pencil scraped busily across his notebook.) 'And I believe Mr Costick quarrelled with his business partner, Mr Poole, about certain . . . well, certain irregularities in the accounts. That's to say, Mr Poole was embezzling money from the firm. Enid . . . that's to say, Enid Costick loves her father, naturally . . . but I think there was some cooling off after she found out he was going to change his will when he got married and cut her off without a penny.'

'Married! Was Costick going to marry, then?'

'Oh yes, sir. He was going to marry Miss Pyke out there. Can't say why. Odd woman. Not right in the head, I sometimes think.'

'Thank you, Mr Gribley. Thank you. You've been most helpful! If you would go and wait with the others . . . and kindly ask the housekeeper to step in here.'

'Well, Sergeant!' exclaimed Farrell, as the dwarf clambered out over the broken door. 'There's a whole pack of motives! What have we got? Read out your notes!'

Sergeant Troughton read out: 'Mr Neville Costick in debt, £1,000 and couldn't pay.

– Mrs Beattie fired for pilfering.

– Mr Wembley Poole caught embezzling from the business.

– Enid Costick cut out of will.

– Miss Pyke engaged to be married to the deceased.'

'So we can rule *her* out, Sergeant. The daughter, on the other hand, would gain by killing him before he changed his will. She's quite tall, isn't she?'

'Pretty tall, sir,' said Sergeant Troughton thoughtfully, moving across to the roll-top desk. He put on his uniform gloves and carefully raised the lid and began searching the various compartments. The blotter was stained a deep, unpleasant red. 'In my limited experience, sir, these Biedermeier desks sometimes have . . . ah yes . . . a trigger which releases . . . a secret compartment. Yes. Here it is.' He took out a pencil drawer and pressed a length of wooden beading, and a drawer sprang open spilling loose papers across the bloodstain.

'Let me see!' exclaimed the inspector. 'Don't go smudging fingerprints, Sergeant!'

'No sir. Sorry sir. This one seems to be a letter from a detective agency, sir, concerning Miss Pyke. It seems Mr Costick was checking up on his future bride.'

Inspector Farrell looked sulky. 'Let that be a lesson to you, boy. Never eliminate anyone from an investigation till you're sure.'

'No sir. Thank you sir.'

'Ah! Mrs Beattie! Come in. I have some questions to ask you about the sherry . . .'

The housekeeper denied categorically that she had ever drunk Mr Costick's sherry or stolen so much as a teaspoon. She also denied Mr Costick had given her the sack. 'He were a right misery and a money-lender, but 'e never had cause to complain about my work nor my honesty, and that's God's own truth!'

'Hmm,' said Farrell when she had gone. 'Of course she can afford to lie now Costick's dead.'

Miss Pyke, the dead man's fiancée said, 'That's right! That's right! We were engaged to be married. It was all going to be wonderful and now . . . and now . . . oh!' Another burst of tears rubbed out her sentence.

The inspector sat back, unmoved, and with a small sardonic smile on his lips. 'Were you aware that your betrothed employed a private detective to look into your past, Miss Pyke . . . or should I say *Mrs* Pyke? These papers from Mr Costick's desk make very interesting reading, madam.'

The handkerchief fell to the floor. The tearful face froze into a pallid mask. 'So. What's to say? You've found me out. When he read that, it was as if he changed into somebody else. Do you know what? He didn't just call off the wedding. Oh no! That I could have understood. That I could have stood. But he wanted money! He wanted money to keep quiet about my . . . my little secret. He said, "You've got money enough," he said. "That's the only reason I was going to marry you, after all." I'm glad he's dead. I'm glad! I'm glad! If someone hadn't murdered him, I would've!'

The sergeant recovered her handkerchief from under

the table and asked her to wait with the others in the living room. As he returned from helping her across the wreckage of the door, his commanding officer said, 'That's the one, then. She did it.'

'If you say so, sir,' said the sergeant, putting on his heavy black gloves again and delicately opening each long drawer of the desk in turn. He lifted out some old accounts books and cheque-books torn in half so that only the stubs remained. 'But haven't you often told me, sir: once a blackmailer, always a blackmailer.' He thumbed through the stubs. 'Perhaps . . . WP. Yes and here it is again: WP. A paying-in every four weeks with the initials WP against it. Do you suppose Mr Costick might have been blackmailing Mr Wembley Poole over the matter of the embezzlement?'

Inspector Farrell slapped his thighs. 'By Jove, Troughton!' Then he sobered himself and dusted his jacket-front thoughtfully, studiously. 'And he's tall enough, of course. Ask Mr Poole if he would be so good as to honour me with his presence,' he said, in a voice steeled with sardonic wit.

Wembley Poole stumbled into the room – a man built like a side of beef, with a red face and a loud wheeze.

'Tell me, sir,' said Farrell succinctly. 'Is it true that the dead man was blackmailing you?'

It took time to break down the man's outraged bluster, but at last Farrell reduced Poole to a panting, wheezing heap of remorse. 'Yes. True,' admitted Poole, his breath only sufficient for telegraphic sentences. 'Didn't kill'm though!'

'Wembley Poole, I arrest you for the . . .' The inspector's dignified delivery of the formal arrest was interrupted by his sergeant's sudden, hacking cough.

'If I might have a word, sir.'

'Not now, Sergeant, I'm arresting . . .'

'Just a little query about procedure, sir.'

Flustered, Inspector Farrell told Wembley Poole to wait outside, and would not let him out of sight until two burly police constables were seated on either side of Poole on the chintz sofa. Back in the office, it was possible still to hear the laboured, wheezy breathing coming from the living room.

'Well, Sergeant?' snapped Farrell.

'I was just wondering, sir, how Mr Poole got out of the room after murdering his blackmailer. The door was locked on the inside, you see, when the body was found . . . well, I don't need to remind you of that, sir, of course.'

The inspector's eyes gleamed and he sprang up athletically. 'I've worked all that out, Sergeant! He hid until the body was discovered, then crept out in all the noise and confusion!'

'Hid where, sir?'

'Here, Troughton!' and he dived behind the curtains.

'Mr Poole is a man of considerable bulk, sir,' said the sergeant, looking sceptically at the big bulge of the inspector's stomach through the curtain, and the pair of black socks and shoes still showing.

'Well . . . *here*, then,' said Farrell irritably, sprinting over to an ornamental Chinese screen and disappearing behind it. 'Stand by the door as if you just came in. Can you see me now?'

'No sir . . . '

'Well then! That wraps it up.'

'. . . but I think I might hear Mr Poole's laboured breathing coming into a silent room, as it were.'

'Damn!'

The inspector re-emerged and flopped down in a threadbare, dusty armchair. 'Damn!' he said again, and added sulkily, 'Well that's how *someone* did it . . . unless, of course, we're dealing with a conspiracy here. Everybody has motives except Gribley.'

'Hmm,' said Sergeant Troughton doubtfully. He had returned to the roll-top desk, and he took a small magnifying glass out of his pocket. 'The forensic department may be useful, sir. I took the liberty of telephoning them when I found these hairs earlier on.'

'*Hairs*! It'll be rabbits next! Come away from that confounded desk, Sergeant. You'll mess up all the clues . . .'

'Yes sir. Very good, sir.'

'What hairs?'

'Hairs caught on the inside of the lock mechanism, sir. Not Mr Costick's colour. And of course there's blood *inside* the desk compartment, sir, indicating that the roll-top lid was open when the murder was committed, not shut as it was when the body was found.'

'An interesting line of argument, Sergeant,' said Farrell, rubbing his jaw in a gesture of profound thought. It rather contradicted the unhappy look in his eyes. 'Go on, Sergeant.'

'Perhaps you'd like to have Mr Gribley back in now, sir?'

'The dwarf? But he's the only one who actually *liked* Costick!'

'We only have his word for that, sir.'

'And he was well paid!'

'So he says, sir, although the accounts books from the desk show no weekly or monthly outgoings on wages. In fact, it rather looks as if Mr Gribley worked for nothing at all.'

'Huh?'

When the sergeant went to the door and called out Gribley's name, the little secretary came scurrying eagerly in response, and written on his face was an almost dog-like keenness to be of service. He gazed at Farrell expectantly. Farrell stared back and said, 'Ah, yes. Mr Gribley. Hmm.' There was an embarrassed silence.

'The Inspector has asked me to run over one or two points with you, sir,' said Sergeant Troughton.

'Ah! Yes! Absolutely,' said the inspector and, pressing his fingertips together and slumping into a Sherlock-Holmesian attitude in the armchair, the inspector prepared to listen. 'Go ahead, Sergeant.'

'As Mr Costick's secretary, you must have been well acquainted with his desk, Mr Gribley. I mean he probably sent you to it from time to time to fetch papers, accounting books and so on.'

'From the drawers, sir, yes. The top's a different matter, of course, given my size, sir.'

'But surely, Mr Gribley, with the use of a chair . . .'

'Well maybe . . . but I didn't, I mean he didn't . . . send me to the desk, I mean.'

'Not often, you mean to say. Otherwise how could there be strands of your hair caught in the lock, sir? The Inspector wonders.'

Gribley clapped a hand to his head. 'Well sir. Yes. On occasions maybe.'

'Well perhaps only the once, eh, Mr Gribley?' The sergeant pushed the chair hard up against the bureau and indicated that Gribley should show him. The dwarf clambered up on to the chair and leaned across on to the open desk-top. 'So that to reach the secret compartment, Mr Gribley, you would virtually have to pull yourself on to the writing surface.'

'Secret compartment? I don't know nothing about no secret compartment. Is there one? I'm sure I never saw dear old Mr Costick open no secret compartment. I certainly never . . .'

'Well, to open the pencil drawer, then,' said the sergeant, cutting in.

To open the pencil drawer (which concealed the secret latch) Gribley had to rest one knee on the blotter and lean forward like a mountaineer on a tricky escarpment.

'Now just supposing you were in that position when you heard Mr Costick coming. Supposing you had reason to think Mr Costick would be pretty annoyed to find you rifling his desk . . . '

'*Rifling his desk? Never!*'

'For what? Some unpleasant piece of information about you? Something which obliged you to work for Costick for no wages, month in, month out?'

'He paid me! I told you he paid me well!'

'Not according to the accounts books. And you haven't answered my . . . the Inspector's question yet. Suppose you were disturbed in this . . . *awkward* position. Would it not be easier to go forward than to go back – that's to say climb inside and shut the lid rather than jump down with all the noise and risk of discovery that would cause?'

'You're talking rubbish! You don't know what you're talking about. *You* believe me, don't you, Inspector. It's just him saying all this!'

'Then Mr Costick came in,' said Sergeant Troughton, lapsing suddenly into the past tense. 'He locked the door behind him, not wanting to be disturbed, and found his desk . . . closed, just as it had been when he left it. You hoped he had no need to go to his desk. If he had simply gone to the lower drawers or the filing cabinet, or made a telephone call, and then gone out again, he would be alive now, wouldn't he, Mr Gribley? But unfortunately he wanted something out of the top compartment. He raised the lid – couldn't make out what he was seeing for a moment, I daresay. Then you struck out with the letter-opener lying on the blotter. His chest was only inches away. It was easy, wasn't it, Mr Gribley?'

'No! No! No! I didn't! It was Poole . . . or the woman . . . or the daughter, not me!'

'Then you heard Mrs Beattie knocking at the door, and knowing you could not escape from the room, you closed the roll-top lid again and waited – *inside the desk* – while the door was broken down, the body discovered and everybody present rushed out of the room in their haste to contact the police. During that time you destroyed whatever document it was Costick was using to blackmail you. Only when the room was empty did you climb out, close the desk and join the general confusion outside. The housekeeper was never fired, was she, sir? Nor was Costick's daughter cut out of the will. You just wished us to have a nice choice of suspects. But you gave us too many, Mr Gribley. You should have stuck at one or two. That's what first made the Inspector suspicious, Mr Gribley . . . And now he would like to hear what you have to say.'

'Nothing! I've got nothing to say!' cried the dwarf. 'Not till I've seen my lawyer!' Standing up in the open desk, he was taller than Poole, taller than Neville Costick, taller than the sergeant or the inspector who rose now from his chair like the wrath of Judgement Day.

'Timothy Gribley! I arrest you for the murder of Angus Costick. Call for secure transport, Sergeant.'

The distant drone of sirens announced the arrival of a police van which Sergeant Troughton had taken the liberty of summoning an hour before. The prisoner was taken into custody – a dark, lonely custody given the great height of prison windows.

'Put the items of evidence into plastic bags and mark the bags carefully, Sergeant,' said Inspector Farrell, brushing the palms of his hands together in a gesture of satisfaction.

'Yes sir.'

'Deduction, Troughton. That's what it's all about. Slow, painstaking deduction. You have to be methodical in this game, Sergeant. It's no good jumping to hasty conclusions. You'll learn that if you ever go on to the criminal detection side.'

'Yes sir. Thank you, sir.'

'That's all right, Sergeant. I don't mind giving young officers the odd tip from time to time. And if you want any advice, you just come to me and ask.'

'Thank you kindly, sir. I'll bear it in mind.'

* * *

'That's typical of CID,' said one of the police constables, no longer perched on the horsehair sofa.

'Amazing though. Who'd've thought it?' said his

colleague. Together they ran fingers tender with awe over the dull, scratched wood and lifted the squeaky, slatted roll-top and dabbed their fingers across the stained blotter. 'Who'd've thought it?' said the constable a second time, then returned grudgingly to his notebook and his unfinished taking-down of details. 'Sorry. Your name again, sir?' he asked MCC, but this time with friendly respect.

Just at that moment, he noticed Uncle Clive lurking awkwardly in the doorway of the living room, caught between the telephoning inspector and his uniformed officers. 'Here! I know you! You're the one we pulled in for breaching the peace and assault and battery down by the railway station! Knocked some poor old geezer down for accidentally jagging you in the head with his umbrella!'

'Uncle Clive!' exclaimed Ailsa, and Mrs Povey gave another shrill, hysterical laugh.

'I told you then, we can do without your sort down here,' the constable went on. 'You want to take your bar-room brawling back up north with you. You'll find we've got no patience with it down here.'

Short, round and forward-tilting like a howitzer, the detective inspector burst from the living room. 'It's Latvian Johnny, all right. No time to lose. We'll be in touch, sir. We're much obliged to you, sir. Much obliged. We'll have to take the gear, of course. Sorry about that. Your loss, I'm afraid. And we'll need you to give evidence, maybe. Jump to it, lads. It's that row of books, the stuffed fish and the bookcase. Into the motor. Right load of old junk if you ask me, but the owner's kicking up one hell of a stink wanting it back. Stolen a month ago from old Birdman Sweeney's luxury penthouse . . . Yes, I know he's a gangster and you know he's a gangster, we all know he's a gangster, but sometimes it's the unhappy lot of a policeman to find a gangster's stolen fish and return it to him as if he were a law-abiding, tax-paying citizen. And who's the loser? Nice people like you here. You go along and buy the junk with your hard-earned money, and we come and take it off you and give it back to Birdman Sweeney. I wonder sometimes. I really wonder sometimes.' And with this philosophical lament, and with a stuffed salmon under his arm, the inspector rushed out to his squad car. The constables followed behind, one with a black plastic sack full of books, the other with a small bookcase. The shop seemed to sag and sigh when they were gone.

Half an hour later, Uncle Clive clattered down the stairs with his suitcase and barged his way recklessly, wreckingly, to the door. 'Must you be going?' Mrs Povey called after him. But he only hunched his shoulders higher towards his alpine hat and shot a look of murderous loathing at the man in cricket flannels and green corduroy jacket.

'There are them as know when to leave,' he said, 'and there are them as don't!'

CHAPTER TEN

THE WOODEN CHEST: A STORY OF BETRAYAL

'That's interesting,' said MCC, standing away from the tall bookshelves to see higher. 'How did that one get up there?'

'Oh, Mum rearranged some. I don't know why. Perhaps she thought they were unsuitable for me to read.'

Ailsa had taken to reading a lot, lately. No sooner did she get home from school than she got changed, brushed her hair and curled up with a novel on the horsehair sofa in the shop. She and MCC did not talk much, but she liked being near him. She had a great hankering to talk about him at school and yet, at the same time, a strong intuition that she should not. She was extremely excitable – something she put down to the day by day survival of the family business. Like a tightrope walker crossing Niagara Falls on a piece of string, Povey's Antiquary struggled on, just balancing its debts against its earnings and never quite plunging into the abyss of bankruptcy. It was thrilling to watch. This was undoubtedly why Ailsa's heart seemed always to be in her mouth lately. Undoubtedly.

'Or me,' said MCC.

'Pardon?'

'Or maybe your mother thought some of the books were unsuitable for *me* to read.'

'Get one down and see.'

'Dear me. I don't think I should. I'm sure Mrs Povey had some good reason . . .'

Not for the first time, Ailsa looked at him and wondered how old he was. Generally speaking the world could be dealt, like a pack of cards, into two stacks – people like her mother and people like her – with a few miscellaneous babies and old people on the discard pile. Try as she might, she could not put an age to Mr Berkshire. He was much older than her, of course, but far younger than her mother. In fact there did not seem to be enough years between her age and her mother's age to fit in all the ages MCC Berkshire might be. And was he her ally or her mother's? Could people really be both?

She fetched the step-ladder and climbed it herself to inspect the books on the topmost shelf. There were paperbacks, hardbacks, softbacks and even leather-bound ones with gold tooling: *Love Among the Lilacs*, *Romance on the Rialto*, *The Baron's Bride*, *A Summer Wedding*, *For the Hand of a Princess* . . .

'They're all soft romances,' she said disappointedly.

'You don't like romances?' he asked steadying the ladder.

'I prefer horse stories. Do you know any good horse stories?'

'Can't say I do, honestly.'

'Know any good romances, then?' she asked brightly.

He looked up at her with his head on one side, with eyes much bigger and darker than eyes ought to be, and said, 'Only sad ones, Ailsa.' Then he turned his back and sat down on the bottom rung of the ladder and rested his head in his hands. 'There was once a man who travelled further afield than he should, to a place he didn't know, and there he found himself a job and a home and a beautiful girl, all under the one roof. The girl was young, but alas the traveller was far from the days of his youth and all he carried in his pack was a book of stories . . .' At the sight of Mrs Povey standing in the doorway, MCC broke off guiltily.

'And just what are you selling, and to whom?' said Ailsa's mother.

A customer of whom none of them had been aware slumped into view from the tallboy and empty picture frames. He was a picture of dejection, in a long black mac which trailed open to show a black pullover and black trousers. The only colour about him was the university scarf which hung round his neck like the bloodstains of a murdered rainbow – and his eyes which were bloodshot, perhaps from prolonged weeping. 'Can someone tell me about this wooden chest?' he enquired in a voice drenched in tragedy, and threw back a lock of hair off his forehead like a man in front of the firing squad casting aside the blindfold.

'Go on, MCC,' said Ailsa.

'Go on, Mr Berkshire,' said Mrs Povey.

MCC breathed deeply and lifted his head out of his hands. He knew the chest well enough. 'Late sixteenth century,' he said. 'Oak. Note the carving depicting a hunting scene on all four sides. It's the oldest thing in the shop. Not rare exactly. The back hinges are missing and the hasps don't fasten – that's to say the lid falls off if you open it. But it's a nice little historical item. A hundred and twenty if you want it.'

'*MCC!*' exclaimed Ailsa and her mother, both outraged by this stark, bald honesty.

'Ah, you mean its *story*,' said MCC bitterly. Then he fetched out a smile, much as a condemned and leaky battleship might hang out flags overall on its last rusty voyage to the breaker's yard.

* * *

'Open up in the name of the Queen! Open, I say!'

Chickens scattered noisily across the yard. The horses behind him tossed their heads and milled uneasily to and fro, and he beat with his fist on the door. Somewhere in the house a dog began to bark – an upper window opened and a housemaid stared down at them before pulling in her head again. There was a scuffling of feet in the hallway, but Eliott continued to beat remorselessly on the door. 'You!' he shouted at a soldier. 'Break down this door!'

'Oh come now – no need for that, surely!' Magistrate Pole had been fetched to witness the house search and to give authority to any arrests about to be made, but whether he liked the business was another matter. He took no relish in catching Roman Catholics, especially when they were his neighbours, like the good Widow Tyford. No wonder folk called this zealous young man 'Priestcatcher' Eliott: he loved his work.

'No need, Magistrate? No need? You don't know these Papists. They're cunning. Give them five minutes and they can hide away a whole army of priests and mask even the smell of them!' But there was no need to break down the door. The inner bolt slid back and there stood Widow Tyford, her lace cap slightly awry and her face flushed and her eyes round with ill-concealed fright. 'What's the matter, sirs? Oh, what's the matter? What do you want with us?'

Eliott pushed past her into the house, and his soldiers followed him, flinging open cupboard doors and overturning tables. The magistrate sidled in awkwardly from the yard, removing his hat. 'Good day to you, Mistress Tyford, I repent this sorely, but the Queen . . . the Act . . . These informers . . . be comforted, lady and show patience. Master Eliott here has it in his head . . .'

He let the words trail away as Eliott pushed between them and blared into the face of the widow. 'We have information that a papist mass has been held here today by a priest – a Jesuit – expressly against the law of the land. Where have you hidden your *Jesuit*, woman?' He said the word as if it fouled his mouth to speak it.

The old lady straightened her cap. 'The Queen's law

forbids the preaching and practice of the Old Faith, sir. Only God may read in my heart what I think to that, but it seems to me that any gentleman who calls himself a Christian might be ashamed to act so unmannerly in a poor woman's house. Search if you must, then leave my home, sir.'

Eliott was not rebuked. He harried his soldiers through the house, pointing them towards the chimney, the beds, the bread oven, the loft. They went to it with pikes, rattling the sharp blades round the inside of the chimney breast until soot cascaded out across the floor. They jabbed the blades through an alcove curtain and left it gashed to tatters. They drove their pikes under the bed; they threw open the linen press and, after pulling out a sheet or two, drove a pike through the remainder of the linen. They drummed with their pike handles against the walls, listening for hollowness, and the Widow Tyford could only follow them about the house, wringing her hands, while her servants and yard-hands flocked round her and shouted angry protests at the soldiers. 'For shame!' 'For God's charity!' 'Leave off, for pity's sake!' 'Haven't you persecuted us enough already?' It was not the first time Priestcatcher Eliott had raided the farmhouse.

As Widow Tyford reached the head of the stairs, she saw the linen press gaping open, the bed upended, and the three armed soldiers beating the wall and, giving a short, choked cry, she staggered in a swoon and it was all her maidservant could do to shut the chest lid and lay her mistress unconscious across it. A malevolent glint of assurance lit the eyes of Priestcatcher Eliott: 'Fetch the sledge-hammer. I believe we are searching close to the mark!'

A terrible silence fell over the house, split at last by the blows of the hammer. The house itself seemed to groan at the blows, as the bricks stove inwards on a mean little cavity. But it was not the loam or bricks that cried out, only the man concealed inside the priesthole as flying bricks struck him in the face and body.

They pulled out the Jesuit covered in brickdust and blood, and had manhandled him down the staircase before the Widow Tyford regained consciousness. She woke to find Eliott's face thrust close to hers: 'For the receiving and concealing of a Roman Catholic priest, a fine of one hundred pounds. For the hearing of a Roman Catholic mass,' and he shook a poor crust of bread and an empty goblet in her face, 'a fine of twenty pounds. I trust, Magistrate, that I am correct in my knowledge of the law? I have had much practice in *this* house, have I not, mistress? Though I have never taken their ferret of a priest before. This is a good day's work.'

'You may be right in your knowledge of the law, Eliott,' muttered Magistrate Pole, 'but as to your Christian charity . . .'

The widow sat up and perched unsteadily on the edge of the carved wooden chest. 'You know full well, Richard Eliott, that your persecution has beggared me and my family. We have no money to call our own. All our savings are gone in fines. We have nothing to pay you with unless you take the sweat from our faces and the blood from our veins. If your soldiers have found above ten farthings as they searched, it will be a thing of amazement to me. You have bled this stone dry, Master Eliott, may God forgive you your tyranny!'

Richard Eliott showed no surprise. 'I have a cart outside, mistress. Let the magistrate be my witness that everything I confiscate is confiscated according to the law. I hereby seize on your goods and chattels in payment of the fine, and if the sale of your furniture does not raise the sum, I shall return to seize on your land and buildings! Your male servants I arrest for aiding the papist spy. You may thank my bounty that you keep your freedom. There are plenty of women of your kind in the Bridewell Prison. Indeed, I shall see you there yet, I dare guess.'

To and fro the soldiers went, emptying the house of its furnishings. The magistrate fretted and twittered about the emptying rooms, protesting at the roughness of the men, but the Widow Tyford sat impassive on the press, her eyes on her lap, her lips moving in a silent prayer. (If Eliott could have proved she was praying in Latin, he would certainly have carried her away in chains.) Only when the soldiers pushed her roughly off the chest and carried it away to the cart in the yard did she break out in loud sobbing and fall on her face along the splintery floor.

Eleanor heard voices in the hall, and ran to greet her betrothed. 'Richard! What brings you here, sweet friend? Are they the men you command – those men in the yard?'

Richard Eliott revelled in the warmth of the greeting. 'To say true, my business brought me by your door and I thought to bring you a present as I passed.' He snapped his fingers and two soldiers poised at the tail of the cart heaved a carved wooden chest on to their shoulders and brought it into the house. 'A press for your marriage trousseau, mistress, since such you must have now that you have consented to be my wife. Shall it be set down in your chamber?'

Eleanor clutched her fingers to her mouth in an ecstasy of delight. 'Oh my dear Richard! Yes, yes, have them take it up. What a sweet gentleman you are indeed to be mindful of me when you are about your business. I shall soon believe that you love me,' she added flirtingly.

'Oh believe it, lady! Believe it! My heart is yours entirely and you are never far from my mind working or waking, sleeping or stirring.'

'But where does it come from? Where did you find it? Such pretty carving!' she exclaimed, as the chest rocked and jarred its way up the narrow stairs. 'Are you escort to a cargo of furniture, my dear?'

'Confiscated!' he declared proudly. 'I come from

raiding a den of heretic Catholics where I cornered a foul Jesuit priest. See him bound there in the cart!'

Eleanor peeped nervously past her fiancé at the black-clothed prisoner wedged between the furniture. 'Oh well done, Richard! Good work! Do you hear that, Mother! Richard has caught a Jesuit!'

Eliott coloured deeply with pride. 'I confiscated the furniture from that den of vice and wickedness – but I paid in cash for the press: I would not have you think I pilfered it from the State!'

'I would never think that, Richard! Indeed I would not. You are a kind, good, honourable man and I thank God that he has brought me such a husband.'

Much as he would like to have stayed, Richard Eliott's duties urged him to hurry away with his soldiers and his prisoner and his confiscated goods, and Eleanor hurried upstairs to rejoice in the gift from her betrothed. A press for her trousseau! What a dear, chivalric thought, and on a day when he had other such important work in hand! She ran her fingers over the birds and animals carved in oak. The hasps were undone. There was no padlock to it. She lifted the lid and found that it was not empty. 'Linen too!' After all, linen is an important beginning to any bride's home-making. She fingered the sheets, her heart stuffed with tender sentiments towards her beloved Richard.

Then she drew back the top sheet and found the one below red with wet blood.

The horror snatched her breath away. As she jumped back, she caught her foot in her gown and stumbled and sat down. Her eyes were on a level now with the press as the bloodstained sheet was thrown back over the side and an elbow flapped vainly to hook itself over the rim and a bloody hand dropped limply on to her knee.

'Magna est veritas et praevalebit . . . Non omnis moriar . . . Water, for the love of God.'

She thought to slam the lid and run for help. But to reach the lid she would have to lean across the man in the press. Her legs seemed to have turned to water, and every time she tried to rise, her treacherous petticoats ensnared her feet and overbalanced her. She tried to scream, but it was as though her vocal cords had been plucked out. The question kept struggling for a place in her mind: Why had Richard presented her with a man's body in a chest? It must have some meaning. She stared at the hand on her knee and it gradually tightened into a fist, clasping her dress.

'God forgive me for a coward, but I fear to die in a linen press. May I not be shriven!' A head emerged a few inches from her own. It was a face of absurdly childlike innocence, not above twenty years old. The boy looked about him in astonishment. 'What is this place?'

'Who are you?'

'Who are *you*?'

'This is my chamber.'

'Then why am I in it?'

'That's what I asked you!'

The conversation congealed again, like a stream refreezing into ice. They stared at each other until gradually understanding dawned on Eleanor. 'You were hiding in the chest. You're a Roman Catholic! You're a Jesuit!'

'A member of the Society of Jesus, yes mistress.' His eyes gleamed with pride.

'But you were captured! I saw a priest in the cart yonder! Richard captured you!'

This news struck horror into the young man. 'Ah! Father Hart was taken, then? God be with him. God give him patience to make a good end . . . He was so much better hidden than I! He was so much better a man than I! He converted me to the True Faith. He was one of the Mission of Fifteen sent by the Holy Father himself from Rheims. I was nothing but the idle son of a good Catholic house until Father Hart came to us and preached. I begged him to admit me to the Society and he agreed and heard my vows – and now he's taken and I'm not!' He made an effort to climb out of the press, but slumped back, panting with pain and frustration.

'How came you hurt?' she whispered, thinking he had perhaps attempted suicide, that most unforgivable of sins. Who knew what these devilish spies might not do?

'The pikemen. They drove pikes into the chest. I pray their idleness in searching has delivered me into gentler hands. Are you a friend of the Widow Tyford? Did she convey me here? Am I to escape after all?' Large tears filled the young man's eyes at the shock of sudden hope.

'No! Widow Tyford is a Catholic! We never speak her name in this house!'

The realization that he was in the hands of a Protestant after all dealt the boy a bitter blow. 'So be it,' he said and mumbled something in Latin.

'Here. Lean on me. You must lie on the bed while I fetch a surgeon to you.' Eleanor said this as coldly as possible and felt quite polluted by the touch of his heretic hand on her shoulder, more so by the blessing he clumsily offered her with one bloodstained hand as she helped him to the bed.

As she turned to go she asked, 'What will become of the Jesuit – the other one, I mean?'

'He will be put to the rack – as if the rack could stretch the law of God out of its true shape! But he will never recant! He will never betray his mission! And if his soul is patient and his tormentors merciful, he will be hanged soon.'

'No!'

'Of course.' The Jesuit seemed puzzled by her surprise. 'That antichrist Eliott – 'Priestcatcher' they call him – he's sent four saints to the rack and the rope this very year . . . Now I must steady my mind to bear my own fate patiently.'

She was by the door now. 'What is your name, Jesuit?'

'Peter . . . Father Kirby, mistress,' said the boy, who was so new to his vows as to forget his brotherly title now and then.

'I shall go now,' she said, though her hand rested on the doorhandle for a long long time.

Five minutes later she returned with a ewer and basin and set to tearing into shreds the sheets which had come in the oak press.

Eliott laughed at the informer. He laughed at him and then he knocked him down and had him thrown in gaol for trying to pervert the course of justice. He kept the grin on his face afterwards. It gave the lie to a horrible coldness that pressed against his heart.

Eliott slapped his palms on his thighs decisively. He would ride over to Eleanor's house at once and tell her the comic business of the informer. Eleanor a covert Catholic! Ha! Eleanor shielding a priest! It was the funniest thing he had heard for a year. He laughed out loud to prove it.

He rode at full tilt, wanting to surprise Eleanor: it is always fun to startle a kitten. He was so impatient to tell her the joke that his wait at the door seemed endless. He banged loudly.

Then Eleanor's mother opened the door. She must have mistaken him for someone else in the bright sunlight, for she went ashy pale. He cut short his greeting and hurried by her, explaining, 'The strangest thing, mistress! Such merriment we had this morning! I must tell it to Eleanor before the mirth splits me!' He looked around the living room, but there was no sign of Eleanor – only a pair of candles smoking on the table and Eleanor's father staring at him as if he were some strange intruder. 'Forgive me if I startle you, sir. Where's my lady?' (Candles lit in sunlight?)

'I . . . I don't know.'

So Richard leapt up the stairs and knocked on her

chamber door. 'Good morrow, sweet lady. Such merriment we had this morning . . .'

She snatched the door open and gazed up into his face as if he were a fiend out of Hell. His heart stumbled in its beat. Such a look! 'Did I affright you, maid?'

'Yes. Yes, yes, you affrighted me, Master Eliott. What do you want?'

So uncivil? He eased his way into her room. 'Such merriment we had this morning . . .' he began again to say. 'A villain came and informed that your family was a nest of covert Catholics, ha! ha!, that you even had a Jesuit hidden away in this house of papism and heard mass and were . . . preached to . . . by . . .' His sentence bled to a stop as though it had been pressed to death by the weight of his heart. For out of the closed chest, between lid and side, hung a corner of black cloth. As his eyes rested on it, it was slowly drawn inside and disappeared. She saw his eyes go to the chest.

'Is your trousseau almost ready, mistress?' He stepped towards the press.

She darted in front of him, shielding the press. 'Almost ready, my lord . . . But it is unlucky for a bridegroom to see his bride's wedding clothes before time.'

Eliott's face broke into a snarl. '*Why, you mean to wear black, lady?*' And pushing her aside, he threw open the lid and bodily lifted out the man hidden inside.

For a minute, for a lifetime, the whole house fell silent. The door creaked, and when it swung open Eleanor's parents stood outside, the wife clinging to her husband. They were a party to the treachery.

Richard Eliott did not want to speak. He had no words in his head. But it seemed that if he did not, no new word would ever be spoken again: the world would lapse into everlasting silence. 'Who . . . are . . . you?' he mouthed into the face of the young man whom he held by the revers of his black gown. The boy dropped his eyes.

'He is my lover,' said Eleanor with slow deliberation. 'I cannot marry you, Richard. I do not love you. I love this man and we mean to marry. So kindly unhand my betrothed,' and she went and put her hand through Father Kirby's arm.

'I don't believe you, mistress,' said Eliott.

'Why else should a young man be hidden in my chamber, hidden from you? I vow to you, he's slept in this chamber every night for two months and this I swear to.'

'He's a priest, lady – a filthy, heretical, soul-stealing Jesuit – and you are a Catholic viper out of a brood of Catholic vipers.'

She maintained her calm better. 'Which would be worse, Richard? That this man was my lover or that this man was a priest?'

'Oh, a priest, woman! A priest! This is the stuff of damnation!'

She replied calmly, 'Then I see my heart was wise to lose its love for you little by little. For you are a bigot and a mad zealot and love has no place in you.'

'But I love . . .' He seemed torn between fury and desolation. He paused until fury got the upper hand. 'Very well,' he said icily. 'Let a minister of the Church be summoned and let him marry you here, before my face. Then and then only will I believe that this . . . this creature of yours has taken no priestly vows of celibacy and single life. Well, Jesuit? What do you say?'

The boy was trembling so violently that he could not say a word. His mental struggle was written on his face. 'My name is Peter Kirby, sir,' was all he said at last.

Eliott could have called for a bible then and there and got the boy to swear away his faith. But such was the confusion of misery in Priestcatcher Eliott that he was driven on as sure as a man laying a whip to his own back.

The minister came. Eliott saw to it that bride and groom were never left alone together, had no chance for private words, though they sat together on the linen press like gauche sweethearts. But while Eliott told the flustered, dusty minister what was needed of him, Eleanor whispered into Father Kirby's ear, 'Never fear! After, you may escape abroad and return to your order.' The boy only groaned and rocked to and fro and stared into her face as though she were too far away for words to reach.

Richard Eliott never doubted that Kirby was a priest. But he saw his own torture through to the bitter end. No priest he had put to the rack ever suffered as he suffered, forcing his betrothed into marriage with another man, blighting all his hopes and happiness by his own spite. Every minute he hoped to hear the Jesuit break down and confess rather than betray his calling. But Kirby, it seemed, was too afraid, too terrified of torture and hanging to admit to his faith.

When the ceremony ended, Eliott stood with drooping shoulders and a bent head and stared at the gaping wooden press he had intended for his bride's trousseau.

'Are you satisfied, Richard?' asked Eleanor, and the eyes of the whole family told him to go, for he had no more excuse to stay.

When everyone was gone but bride and groom, the boy sat down on the press, buried his head in his hands and burst into tears. 'I have broken my vows! I've betrayed my calling and my order!'

Eleanor began again to reassure him that he had not. 'So long as we do not live together as man and wife . . .' she said. 'And it was no true marriage in the face of God because the minister was not of the true Roman faith! We aren't married at all!'

But he caught hold of her hands and wrung them violently, furiously. 'No! No, you foolish woman! No! Don't you understand yet? For why did I not speak when he forced us to a marriage? For why did I keep silent?'

'For fear, I dare say, but there's no shame in a man feeling . . .'

'Fear? What has a true priest to fear from the likes of Priestcatcher Eliott? When I first came here and I thought you would betray me, I felt no fear, for I had the certainty of a place in Heaven. Oh Eleanor, fear didn't seal up my mouth. It was Love, woman. Love. Because hiding here day by day, preaching to you, watching you and your family grow in the faith, I forgot to love you as a shepherd loves his flock and I found myself loving you as a man loves a wife. I didn't speak because I *wanted* to be wed to you – because I love you above my immortal soul.' He gave a bitter sort of laugh. 'So you have betrayed Eliott. Eliott has betrayed his heart and I have betrayed God. A nice piece of work, lady. A nice piece of work.'

And he kicked the carved wooden press as though it were a living thing and it too could feel pain.

* * *

The lugubrious young gentleman in black was overjoyed. 'I too have had my heart broken!' he declared, slapping his hand to his chest in case they were in any doubt as to where he kept this unfortunate heart. 'I shall place it in my rooms at college and fill it with poetry to HER, and when I die, SHE may have it and WEEP!'

MCC grinned and shook his head and got up smartly from the bottom rung of the step-ladder to help lift the chest. The ladder wobbled, and Ailsa, reaching out a hand to steady herself at the top, pulled a span of books from the top shelf. They tumbled down the steps of the ladder, shedding covers and sleeves.

Ailsa and her mother were presented with the sight of fifty-pound notes cascading like a waterfall from ceiling to floor – one from between every page of an epic hardback romance.

Neither MCC nor the self-absorbed student looked round, but lifted and carried the wooden chest, with considerable grunting and panting, out to the boy's expensive convertible sports car. Before MCC returned, alone, holding the student's cheque, Ailsa and her mother had gathered up seventeen thousand pounds and were both sitting side by side on the *chaise longue* in a state of shock. He put the cheque in the till and, without seeming to glance at the fallen books or the trembling proprietress, said, 'I daresay it's the reason Birdman Sweeney was so very upset about the theft from his luxury penthouse. I suppose you moved the book off the little bookcase that the police took away, and put it on the top shelf when you . . . you reorganized, Mrs Povey. You just happen to have chosen the book where Mr Sweeney kept his small change. I understand he is quite a successful gangster.'

Mrs Povey wanted to return the money at once. She looked up Mr Sweeney in the telephone directory and went directly round to his luxury penthouse. But Mr Sweeney was not there to take back his stolen property.

'Birdman was nicked this morning, missus,' said the butler, peering round the door. 'Latvian Johnny fingered him for the Mons Street job soon as he was collared by the Old Bill. No honour among thieves these days, as I sees it.' And he shut the door in her face.

She was all of a sudden, as MCC put it, unavoidably rich.

CHAPTER ELEVEN

THE LEAD SOLDIER: A STORY OF PRIDE

The following evening Ailsa was lying in bed (wondering why her heart was still in her mouth despite the family business being finally secure) when she heard a noise downstairs which made her unaccountably burst into tears. It was the murmur of conversation between her mother and MCC, and she had not heard a man and woman talking downstairs since her father died. It was a good noise. She had not realized how much she missed it. A person could relax and stop worrying when there were coffee-cups and voices drowning out the tick of the handless clock and the clicking of the basketware chairs in the shop. She was too happy to sleep. She got up, washed her face and sat on the top stair with her knees drawn up to her chin. She could just see MCC over the rim of the stairwell, leaning back against the living-room table.

The first thing she heard dispelled the magic.

'It doesn't mean you have to leave,' said her mother's voice doubtfully.

'But you'd rather I did.'

'It might be better. I mean you could take the money. It's yours by rights. You bought in the book.'

'I don't want the money,' he said impatiently.

'Not even half? Well, we really ought to discuss wages at least. All these weeks you've been working here for nothing.'

MCC disappeared suddenly from sight into the darkened shop and came back and set a single lead toy soldier down in the centre of the table.

'That's off the bric-à-brac table,' said Mrs Povey, puzzled.

'Yes. Can I have it?'

'Of course you can have it. Don't be silly.'

'Thank you,' and he put it into his breast pocket. 'Now I've been paid.'

The next moment he was leaning agitatedly on the arm of Mrs Povey's chair. 'But what's wrong with me? What have you got against me? Is it my age?'

'No! What age are you?'

Ailsa did not catch his answer. 'Well, is it because I have no money?'

'No. I told you, the money's yours if you want it . . . and anyway, I think you knew it was there in the book before we found it.'

'That's it, then! You think I was in league with Latvian Johnny or Birdman Sweeney. Ha! You think I'm a criminal on the run! I swear I'm not!'

'Don't be foolish. Of course I don't think that. It's just that you seem to know a lot more than is quite . . . Look here, MCC. I don't know anything about you. I mean who are your people? Where's your family home? What's your *real* name?'

There was no answer.

'All right, then. Where are your belongings? Don't you own anything? Don't you have a change of clothing anywhere – in a suitcase in a lost property office perhaps? Nothing?'

MCC patted his breast pocket. 'I have this. It's a beginning,' he said hopefully.

'But that's what I'm getting at. Where are your *own* toy soldiers, MCC? What became of the toy-box you had as a child? Where did you grow up? Where were you born? Where's home?'

There was an extremely long pause. MCC took out

the lead soldier again and looked into its blobby, badly painted face. 'My great-grandfather was a general in the Boer War.'

'That's a long way to go back,' said Mrs Povey dubiously. 'Why do I get the feeling you're going to tell me a story?'

'Everyone's personal history is a story,' said MCC woundedly. 'But I won't tell one if you don't want me to.'

'Oh go ahead, do.'

He hesitated, as if collecting the words of the story together in his head. His face took on a great sadness. Mrs Povey clearly saw it, for her old apologetic voice returned just for an instant. 'I only want what's best for Ailsa.'

'That's dangerous,' he said, placing the lead soldier precisely in the centre of the table again.

'I think I know what's best for my own child!' Mrs Povey retorted hotly.

But MCC had squatted down beside the table and had his chin resting on its edge, looking at and beyond the soldier through one eye, as if it were the sights of a rifle. Ailsa crept two stairs lower and forgot that she was trembling from head to foot.

* * *

'You shame me, boy!'

Wellington George Armstrong stood on the hearth-rug between the two winged chairs which flanked the blazing fire. On the one side sat his godfather, silent, smoking; on the other his father, shouting and as red-faced as the King's Scarlet. Wellington George Armstrong bowed his head.

'Stand up straight, boy! Stand to attention!' blared his father. 'I would have thought that uniform had back-bone in it even if you haven't. You shame me in front of your godfather!'

'I don't mean to, sir.'

The General gave a snort of disgust and, taking a pair of walnuts from the dish beside his chair, cracked them together between his two hands, as if he would have liked to do something similar to his son. 'Cowardice! I never thought to give life to a coward! I'd sooner have stayed a bachelor.' He threw the broken shells into the fire where they burned with a series of pistol-crack explosions. The General seemed to take delight in the start his son gave at the noise, thinking it proof of cowardice. What he did not quite realize was that a shard of hot shell had flown off the coals and struck the boy's hand. Wellington George Armstrong bit his lip. The pain of the interview was far greater.

'It isn't that I *don't* want to be in the army, sir. It's just that I *do* want to be a doctor, sir,' he said, but the heat from the fire behind him felt like a foretaste of Hell whose oven doors stood open in wait for him for speaking such blasphemy.

'Don't bandy words with me, boy. You've been bred a soldier, educated for a soldier, dressed as a soldier – and now you say you don't want to be a soldier. You want to be a doctor instead! It's a coward's excuse. It's a callous, wilful slight on me and on your grandfather and on his father before him! Cowardice makes a fellow spiteful. I've seen it in the regiments. A coward's always out to make the unkind cut. Well, you've hurt me, boy, if it gives you any satisfaction. You've really put the blade to my heart and twisted it, boy, and things will never be the same between you and me!'

Wellington George Armstrong was helpless to defend himself. He was well aware that his father's feelings were indeed hurt – that he was probably heart-broken by the announcement that his only son did not want to be a soldier. It had taken every ounce of courage Wellington could muster to speak his mind. That courage had quickly run out. Everything his father said was true: he was a coward. He had come home from the military academy determined to be a doctor instead of a soldier. His trunk was not yet unpacked and his resolve was already weakening.

He had steeled himself against all the wrong things. The beating and the bellowing he had foreseen. But one glimpse of the misery behind his father's bulging eyes and Wellington was all set to surrender, to crumble, to give in and to be a soldier.

If only his godfather would intervene! Wellington had staked all his hopes on Uncle Charlie: he was an army surgeon, after all, and ought to understand. And he had always been sympathetic, in the letters they exchanged during termtime. But now he just sat in the wing-chair and smoked and smiled and smiled and smoked, as Wellington's resolve melted away.

'I'll give you one last chance,' growled the General in a menacing, low voice. 'Give up this fool's idea of yours and swear allegiance to the regiment as you did on your eighth birthday with your poor mother looking on. Your hand on Halbeard! Do it!'

Oh how well Wellington remembered that eighth birthday, that ritual swearing of loyalty to the family regiment, his hands hardly able to reach the stuffed head of a past regimental mascot which hung over the fireplace. Five years later the mangy old hound still glared out into the room, baring its yellow teeth, its glassy eyes dulled by soot from the fire. Halbeard, the dead mascot, growled down at Wellington, full of disappointment. Wellington quailed, his determination and all his hopes ebbing into the hearthrug. He reached up to put his hand into the open, mummified mouth . . .

'Tell you what!' exclaimed Uncle Charlie, lurching forwards in his chair with an amiable grin. 'Why don't you fight it out on the battlefield – the two of you – man to man?'

Father and son stared at him.

'A war game! A game of strategy!' cried Uncle

Charlie, jumping up and heaving aside the furniture until an area of Turkey carpeting emerged, patchy with fading. He pushed Wellington off the hearthrug and threw this in a heap in the middle of the area, declaring, 'Higher ground!' He took off his smoking jacket and flung that down, too, in a bundle. 'Where're your lead soldiers lad? Fetch 'em down!'

Slothful Uncle Charlie had been a source of despair and disappointment to Wellington: Uncle Charlie in braces and high-waisted trousers and shirt unbuttoned at the cuffs, pulling the furniture about the room, was downright alarming, especially since he was, in effect, suggesting a further humiliation for his godson. How could Wellington, at thirteen, beat his esteemed officer father at a game of strategy? There was an element of luck in a war game, but not one large enough. Never. Wellington looked pleadingly at his godfather, hoping to be spared the game. But however hard he tried, he simply could not catch Uncle Charlie's eye. He fetched his box of lead soldiers. It was the first present his father had ever given him, when he was two, saying, 'One day, Wellington, you'll be a smart soldier like these fellows!'

'I'll call the shots!' cried Uncle Charlie excitedly. To him it all seemed a great joke, and yet it was Wellington's future they were playing for!

Lying on their faces, head to head across the Turkey carpet and rumpled hearthrug, father and son took up the role of enemies. Wellington's toy soldiers were ranged between them, conscripted and forced into the strangest of all battles. The firelight flickered on the flecks of gold paint which made one a major, one a general, and on the unnatural pink of their painted lead faces and on the shiny brass artillery with which Wellington had never played.

'Good! Very good! An excellent idea of yours, Charles,' said the General. 'A battle for self-determination, eh lad? Like some damned Balkan uprising.'

Wellington felt at a further disadvantage being half wedged beneath the sideboard. He struggled to remember the elements of battle plan they had already taught him at school, but his mind was a blank. He could only hope that the dice were kind to him.

Luck gave no quarter. Luck showed no mercy at all.

The General's troops advanced across the Turkey carpet to the foot of the hearthrug, their progress determined by rolls of the dice – three, five, six. They had the mountain to shelter them from Wellington's artillery now, and soon they would take the high ground and pick off Wellington's men with throws of five and six. His troops scurried to the shelter of the smoking jacket, and a sorry, demoralized crew they seemed to Wellington. He could almost see the fear etched on their misshapen lead faces. Beyond the battlescape loomed the huge, fire-bright face of his father, its whiskers as menacing as dark clouds gathering around a setting sun. There was no body – only face: grinning, complacent face.

'Dysentery!' cried Uncle Charlie suddenly and startlingly.

'What?' snapped the General. 'What d'you mean, "dysentery"? Who put dysentery in the rules?'

'No rules in this game,' said Uncle Charlie cheerfully, patrolling the edge of the battlefield on hands and knees. 'No favouritism! Dysentery strikes both sides. What do you do?'

The General herrumphed and reared up off the carpet. He had seen plenty of dysentery on active service. It killed men surer than bullets. But *do*? What *do* about it? 'Don't catch your drift, man. Dig latrines, of course. Dig plenty of latrines.'

'Still, shall we say a twenty per cent mortality?' said Uncle Charlie, knocking down one in five of the General's men. 'And you, Wellington? What would you do?'

Wellington too was confused. He scowled with

bewilderment but he said, 'Set up field hospitals. Give daily equal parts of salt and sugar in boiled water, and dig separate latrines for the men affected and for the men not.'

'*Sugar and salt?* What are you now – a chef?' bawled the General over the summit of the hearthrug.

'Sound medicine. Sound medicine,' Charles interrupted. 'Shall we say five per cent mortality?' and he picked off just two of Wellington's troopers. 'Carry on.'

The set-back soured the General's mood. He ploughed doggedly on up the hearthrug and took the high ground, dominating the battlefield. Charles threw the dice. 'Six!' he declared, and six of Wellington's men lay down to an everlasting sleep on the turkish plush of the plain, far distant from the comforts of their green baize beds in the wooden toy-box. Wellington (who was overblessed with imagination) could almost hear their groans and smell the cordite on their singed and gory jackets. Poor men. To die in such a very poor cause as the wilful disobedience of Wellington George Armstrong, thirteen. Halbeard, the dead, stuffed mascot, grinned down at him with his bared teeth. The noise of the dice rolling sounded as loud as cannon roar.

'Mutiny!'

'Oh now look here, Charles. Don't louse up the game.' The General sat up, his clothes straining, too tight for lying on the floor in comfort. 'Mutiny? Mutiny ain't in the rules.'

'But this ain't a game, General,' said Uncle Charlie, getting to his feet. 'This is the matter of a lifetime. Mutiny. One quarter of your troops mutiny, General. However, they are seized on by the remaining loyal troopers and chained to the munition carts. How do you handle the situation?'

'Shoot them like the dogs they are,' said the General, and it was plain that he too could smell the cordite and hear the rattle of the chains. He picked out his own soldiers as if he were picking maggots out of cake, and threw them disdainfully into the seat of the armchair. 'That's how to deal with a mutiny, lad,' he murmured towards Wellington, having for the moment forgotten that his son did not thirst after such knowledge.

It was Uncle Charlie who seemed now to be holding the only high ground in the living room, for he was standing up and they were lying on their faces at his feet. 'And you, Wellington?' he said.

'A mutiny, too?'

'Don't try to be clever, lad. Just say honestly what you'd do.' Uncle Charlie had stopped smiling.

Wellington was startled by this sudden ferocity into answering truthfully. 'In the middle of a war, sir? I suppose I'd promise to look into their grievances as soon as we got home and beg them to trust and serve me until then.'

'Pah!' The General struck his fist so hard against the floor that Wellington felt the other end of the floorboard lift under his thigh. But Uncle Charlie cut short any tirade by recommencing the battle. 'Wait! Wait!' protested the General. 'You've forgotten to penalize the boy for the mutiny!'

'But he shot none of his men. You shot yours,' said Charles in a quick, businesslike voice. 'Shall we go on?'

Wellington had more men. The General held more ground. The scene was set for a war of attrition dragging on and on, death by death, until a handful of men were left triumphantly huddled on either Hearthrug Hill or Jacket Bluff.

His father's blood running in Wellington's veins began to quicken. A few lucky throws of the dice, another advantage tossed his way by Uncle Charlie, and perhaps he *could* massacre his father's troops and still be left with a man or two standing. He realized, from a pain in his jaw, that he was grinding his teeth hard together. The reason for winning the battle slipped little by little out of his mind. The desire to win, the desire to kill, the desire to humiliate his tyrannical enemy rose up like lava through the seams of a volcano.

'Hostage taken,' said Uncle Charlie.

'Oh d**n you, Charles!' The General uttered an oath Wellington had never even thought he knew. 'More trickery?'

'War's full of trickery, General. You don't need me to tell you that.' Charles had retired to the fireplace and was smoking another cigarette and casually leaning against the mantelpiece, his eyes fixed fast on the battlefield. He was deaf to entreaties, this aloof god of war. 'Your son, General, has been taken hostage. Give up the hill. Surrender. Or his throat will be cut at dawn.'

The General began to cough – huge, convulsive coughs intended to disguise a complete loss of self-control. Across the jagged peak of Hearthrug Hill, he saw the wide, blue, ingenuous eyes of his son watching him, watching him. He must not show the boy an example of weakness. Valour was the very thing at issue. Cowardice was the very crime which had come between father and son. He must give his boy some example of strength – show him the stuff of English pluck. He had to prove how infinitely finer was the profession of a soldier than that of a doctor! 'A British officer's first duty is to his Queen and Country, no matter what the personal cost,' said the General, overloud.

Uncle Charlie cut his speech short and summed up briskly: 'Your son's throat is cut. The hill remains in your hands.'

The General gave an involuntary smile of relief: that hill had come to mean so very much to him.

Uncle Charlie called across the room in a sharp, imperious voice. 'You, Wellington. Your father has been taken hostage. What do you do?'

Wellington lifted his forehead off the carpet. Tears were running down his cheeks and splashing on to the pile of discarded – (dead) – lead soldiers heaped up beside the battlefield. He rested on his father the same look of bewilderment, hurt and reproach that the General had seen in the eyes of young men dying in field-hospital hammocks under fly-blown foreign skies.

'Answer honestly, Wellington!' shouted Uncle Charlie.

So Wellington put out his hand and picked up a fistful of the soldiers from Jacket Bluff and hurled them clumsily, overarm, over the summit of Hearthrug Hill, at his father's big, round, florid face. 'Surrender, of course,' he hissed between shapeless, quivering lips.

A silence filled the room that was broken only by Wellington's quick, agitated breathing and the crack of walnut shells in the firegrate – a sound reminiscent of a cavalry battle over, as the horsemaster tours the field, shooting maimed animals.

Uncle Charlie stepped into the battlefield, his satin-taped trousers and soft leather shoes bringing the whole landscape down to scale. It was, after all, only a yard or two of carpet. He extricated his smoking jacket, letting the last of Wellington's toy soldiers fall on to the carpet pile.

And with his jacket returned to his shoulders, Uncle Charlie returned to his slow, indolent, smiling former self, slouching into an armchair and luxuriantly lighting another cigarette. 'You see what a scurvy soldier he'd make, Tom?' he said conversationally to the man stretched out on the floor. 'Something of the killing instinct missing, don't you know? Gives in to mutineers. Surrenders out of sheer sentiment. Better let him be a doctor hadn't we? He'd be a liability to the Queen.'

The General did not answer. He and his son looked at one another, face to face across the Turkey carpet. All lines of communication were severed, like telegraph wires brought down by shelling. The red glow of the dying fire cast a red gash of light across Wellington's face and throat, and the eyes might just as well have been dead.

Wellington George Armstrong left military academy and ultimately studied medicine. He went to France as a volunteer surgeon at the beginning of the First World War and was killed at the battle of Passchendaele by a mudslide. His father died in bed not long afterwards – of a broken heart, some say.

* * *

Mrs Povey pounced on the conclusion like a cat on to a thread of wool. 'His only son, eh? Died in the trenches? Unmarried? No children?' MCC shrugged. 'Your family tree seems to have died in 1917, then, Mr Berkshire! How extraordinary!'

'I didn't say it was *my* personal history,' said MCC with one of his dazzling, momentary smiles.

Mrs Povey sighed. Her voice, when she spoke again, was weary and harrassed. 'So. Taking your story to heart, I am supposed just to sit back and let Ailsa . . . form an attachment for you.'

'Why not?' said MCC, slipping the toy soldier back into his breast pocket.

Mrs Povey sat forward in her chair and looked him squarely in his huge brown eyes. 'Frankly, Mr Berkshire, because you don't . . .'

CHAPTER TWELVE

THE BED: A STORY OF HORRORS UNSPEAKABLE

Her sentence was never finished.

As dark as the void of Space, MCC's extraordinary eyes, in flight from Mrs Povey's, glanced up the stairwell and caught sight of Ailsa curled up behind the banister.

'Go to bed, Ailsa,' he said, and Mrs Povey swivelled angrily in her chair.

'Go to bed, Ailsa.'

Ailsa withdrew. Below her, after a scurry of cleared coffee-cups, the clicking of light switches, the creak of stairs and the rattle of the great brass bed in the shop, the house settled into silence but for the ticking of the handless clock and the clicking of the basketware chairs.

Next morning, MCC was up and about early. He borrowed a coat that had once belonged to Mr Povey and went to the laundrette to wash his clothes. It was a bright spring day – the last day of April – and he came back sparkling white, his jacket hooked on one finger over his shoulder.

Mrs Povey had washed his clothes often, overnight, but never before had the grass stains entirely disappeared from his knees or his shirt dazzled so pavilion-white. To Ailsa he looked like a white-sailed yacht heeling out of a sunlit wave, black pennants flying and the green ensign limp. But then she had formed a very great attachment for him. For in such matters it makes very little difference ultimately what mothers do or say. She ran to the door and hugged him, to make that much plain to everyone.

But MCC held her at arm's length and looked at her strangely – much as Mrs Povey held a letter when she had not got her reading glasses on. 'I've decided!' he said. 'Today I shall make a sale!'

'And what kind of story will you tell?' asked Ailsa, feeling the empty pockets of his jacket to see which book he was currently reading.

'I haven't decided yet.' He went and stood in front of the bookshelves and read the shelves from left to right, left to right, ceiling to floor. 'What shall it be? Science fiction? No, I loathe science fiction – all pseudo-scientific jargon and airlocks. A spy thriller? No, I'm not intelligent enough for a spy thriller. A Western? No, not for Americans.'

'How do you know they'll be Americans?' said Mrs Povey sharply, but he did not seem to hear.

'Ah yes! A Gothic horror story. That should do nicely.' He pulled a book from the shelf and, falling backwards languidly on to the *chaise longue*, he opened it at page one.

At about half-past eleven, an American couple came into the shop – tourists making a coach trip round the Southern Counties. They owned a shop themselves; it sold old copies of *Superman*, *Dracula*, and *Marvel* comics, just off the Chicago freeway. 'You got old magazines, ma'am?' asked the lady.

'Sorry, no. Only books,' said Mrs Povey.

'They got no magazines, Virgil.'

'Told you they don't, these joints,' said Virgil.

'They got some nice old stuff, Virgil.'

'They do? They got souvenirs, maybe, for the folks back home?'

'You got souvenirs, maybe, for the folks stateside?'

'Well not souvenirs, exactly,' Mrs Povey apologized.

'They don't got souvenirs, Virgil.'

'Sure they got souvenirs, Lindy-Ann. This stuff's English, ain't it? Tell us what's *real English* here, fella?' Virgil was addressing MCC who, as he stood up, looked like the Captain of the English test side going in to field. When MCC spoke, his voice would have raised on tiptoe every blade of grass on the playing fields of Eton, or lifted from the water every dipped oar at Henley Royal Regatta. If he could have done, Virgil would have bought MCC then and there and shipped him home in a crate.

'Everything here is English, sir – this clock, this chair, this table, this whatnot, this tallboy, this firescreen – in fact everything you see here is English . . . except the bed . . . except the bed, except the bed!' And he grasped the brass footrail in both fists, as if the bed might suddenly break free and career away down the high street. 'Except the bed!'

'What's with the bed?' said Virgil.

'Don't ask, sir.'

Virgil was putty in his hands. 'What's with the bed, fella?'

'The story's too terrible to tell . . . too extraordinary, really . . . Too bloodcurdling, anyway.'

'Oh Virgil! He says it's bloodcurdling! Make him tell, honey!' cried Lindy-Ann.

'But it's *your* bed, MCC!' whispered Ailsa, tugging on his sleeve. 'Where will you sleep?'

'Make with the story, brother,' said Virgil. 'Make with the story.'

★ ★ ★

Lightning, like a black-cloaked magician, sawed the night sky in half. It cast a white and sickly glare over the moated grange of Bäddeschløss and set the hounds barking at the utmost tether of their chains. Their slavering jaws chewed at the dank mist which swirled up off the foetid moat, dulling the distant noise of hammering. Fowlstrangler was doing a little carpentry in the basement.

A yellow beam of light from the scullery door shone down the worn stone steps and lit his work – until into that light stepped a figure whose shadow loomed long, thin and black across the hunched manservant.

'Fowlstrangler! I rang and you did not come!'

The squat creature in the basement let his hammer drop and crammed a plait of his long, matted hair into his mouth in craven terror. 'Beg your lordship's pardon, but the cord must've broke what joins the bellpull to the bell.'

'I see it there in your hand, Fowlstrangler. Don't lie to me. What are you doing with it?'

'Building a rack, if it please your lordship.'

'A *wine* rack, Fowlstrangler?'

'No, milord, a rack of the more tormenting and tortuous kind, milord, if it please you!'

The Baron Greefenbludd plucked a shred of cobweb from above the cellar door and ate it thoughtfully. 'It does please me, Fowlstrangler, but I have other things for you to do tonight.'

Astonished at his master's affable mood, the manservant galloped up the steps as fast as his crutch would allow him. 'What is your lordship's pleasure?'

'Ah! My pleasure, yes! The time has come,' declared the Baron, grandly throwing open the doors on to the great hall, carpetless but for the cured skins of eight or nine wildebeest. 'The time has come for me to take a bride, Fowlstrangler.'

'A bride, milord? Of the female, womanish kind, you mean, milord?'

'The very sort, and none more so than the bride I have in mind. Too long has Bäddeschløss been empty of the tender delights of a woman's touch. Too long has it lacked the quiet screaming of little children. Now my eye has chanced upon the ideal bride: Amelia, daughter of the kindly Reverend Lovegood Divine, presently staying at a window-boxed inn in the peaceful tranquillity of a neighbouring valley.'

Baron Greefenbludd wiped soot off the inner recesses of the big fireplace and licked his fingers pensively. 'Prepare a wedding feast, and put sheets on the great bridal bed, Fowlstrangler, then fetch her to me. I have a mind to view her before the ceremony.'

'Very good, milord . . . Might I enquire whether the young lady will be expecting me to call?'

A twitch of irritation crossed the Baron's face. 'It's true that just at present she is unaware of the honour awaiting her – unaware of the favourable impression she has made on my eye. But if she has any misgivings, I can very soon *persuade* her to a liking for me,' and he twisted the fire irons together between his hands as though he were plaiting straw. 'Just bring her to me!' The Baron gave a gesture of impatience which sent Fowlstrangler scurrying through the concealed door and up the spiral stairway to the East Tower of Bäddeschløss Grange.

He drove thirteen cats off the great bridal bed with his crutch and, deciding that the comfort of feathers only encouraged them, stuffed the goosedown mattress out through the arrow-slit window and into the moat below. He then spread hand-woven sheets of silk over the bedsprings, and evicted the rats from under the pillows. Lastly he knotted four solid chains to the four corner-posts of the bed, pulled a large carpet-bag from under the bed, and hopped and tapped his way down the back stairs to the stables.

Wolves howled among the Baron's brick ovens which loomed like petrified haystacks out of the darkened fields. The moon sickened and declined into the arms of a leafless tree. The rocky mountain pass rang hard under the horse's buckled shoes, as Fowlstrangler rode at full tilt, and the icicles tinkled dully and the caverns gaped, full of bear to right and left. The mountains scowled on Fowlstrangler.

But an hour later, he broke through the cage of moonbeams on his way back, the carpet-bag held in his teeth. Tapering screams followed the horse like steam curling around behind a locomotive.

Impatient for his bride, Greefenbludd paced the bedroom, irritably snapping candles out of their candlesticks and eating the wax, like sugar mice, off their tails of wick. At last, the sound of hoofbeats sent him striding to the window. But an unaccustomed shyness drove him to lurk on the windowsill, wrapped in the curtain.

His manservant threw open the door and entered, a bow wave of snow across his chest, and heaved the carpet-bag off his shoulder and on to the bridal bed. The clasps snapped undone and a hand white as milk reached through the opening with pleading fingers. Fowlstrangler drew the woman out by her hair and was just chaining her to the bedstead when Baron Greefenbludd leapt out impatiently with an 'Aha!' which startled the rooks off the picture rail.

The lady's struggles had thrown her long hair across her face, and the Baron, picking her up by the lacings of her bodice, drew back the hair like curtains.

'Uh? . . . You fool, Fowlstrangler!' he cried. 'This is the wrong girl! This is *Evelyn*, the beautiful but bignosed sister of the lovely Amelia Divine. You have brought me the wrong woman, dolt! There is no lack of noses at Bäddeschløss Grange. Noses run in the Greefenbludd family! Take her away!'

Fowlstrangler, one arm folded over his head against the blows, babbled his apologies: 'Such a dark night, your lordship! And these eyes of mine don't see so very well by candlelight. I climbed in at the window and saw a person working at her embroidery and all this hair . . .' And he let the hair trickle through his fingers, absent-mindedly. 'She won't do, then, Master?'

'Take her away and feed her to the sturgeon in the moat!' cried Greefenbludd bitterly. 'Then go back and fetch me the right one.'

Fowlstrangler bit his lip. 'Begging your forgiveness, Master, but if you recall, the sturgeon died – of eating the rowing boat. Another ain't to be had for love nor money!'

The Baron stove in the wardrobe with a single kick of his boot. 'Then set her to work polishing skulls in the family vault. But be quick! I'll not be kept waiting for my future bride!'

With a large sack over his shoulder and an ice-pick and whip in one hand, Fowlstrangler drove the Baron's lightless black carriage back through the Bäddeschløss Pass, through the glowering night and downpour of dark, syrupy rain. The eyes of wild boar glimmered red between the trees, and mudslides slid like reptiles out across the road. Black crêpe cracked itself to tatters behind Fowlstrangler's hat, and black plumes wagged frenziedly above the horse's heads as he whipped them on to greater and greater speed.

An hour later, he returned, the iron-bound wheels striking sparks from the cobbled stableyard of Bäddeschløss Grange as the carriage slewed to a halt. Hurling a brick at the hounds chained beside the door, he bounded lamely up the stairs of the East Tower. The rain streamed off his clothing and down the stone spiral steps behind him, like a waterfall.

The sack across his shoulders bulged and tore, and desperate fingers poked through, and two eyes showed round with fear. The first sight they met was the master of the house squatting on the hearthrug nervously eating coal out of the grate.

Tossing the sack on the bed, Fowlstrangler ripped it asunder with a triumphant flourish. 'Your bride, milord!'

'Idiot! Fool! Bungler! What's this? This is the kindly Reverend Lovegood Divine, *father* of the adored Amelia! What's the matter with you, Fowlstrangler? I burn with impatience and you bring me this!' And he picked up his manservant by the head and threw him against the wall. 'Feed him to the vampire bats, then fetch me the bride of my desire!'

Fowlstrangler sheltered under a table and wailed, 'Forgive me! The inn was all in darkness! Everyone had gone to bed, Master! I listened at each bedroom door, but these ears of mine can't judge so well between the breathing of a man and the breathing of a woman . . . And begging your pardon, milord, but the vampire bats are off their feed again.'

'So set him to digging graves! Then fetch me the lovely Amelia – and hurry! Don't try my patience too far!'

So Fowlstrangler returned to the stables and harnessed the sleigh. Its runners scored sharp grooves across the cobbles of Bäddeschløss Grange with a noise like a cut-throat razor. Rain, hail, snow and grit stood in wind-twirled columns along the roadside, but nothing could halt Fowlstrangler in his determination to do the bidding of his master. Though avalanches fell from the angry peaks until the horses struggled and swam chest-deep through rubble and snow, he finally reached the inn, pretty with window-boxes, sheltering in the peaceful neighbouring valley.

He hacked through the wooden props which shored up the inn on the mountainside, and saw it tumble down, all planks and splinters . . . 'Rats!' he said, when it fell on top of his sleigh.

So it was almost dawn before Fowlstrangler, on foot, reached Bäddeschløss Grange again, a padlocked chest on his back and his crutch worn down to a mere twig. He found his lord and master on the borders of the estate: his eagerness had brought him out in his shirtsleeves to gobble sheep's wool off the barbed wire. He gambolled eagerly alongside his servant, pawing the lid of the chest with eager hands. They strained, shoulder-to-shoulder, through the door of the East Tower. They bounded up the spiral stairs, Greefenbludd treading on Fowlstrangler's fingers. The chest was thrown down on the bridal bed, where the Baron impatiently dismantled it by rending out each iron nail with his teeth. 'At last! At last! Let me lay eyes and hands on my long-awaited . . . *Fowlstrangler*!'

'Is there something, milord?'

'Fowlstrangler, you loon! You booby! You dolt! You jobbernowl blunderhead! Tell me before I die in ignorance – where is the lovely Amelia and *why have you brought me a window-box*?' And he picked up his manservant and pushed him out through the arrow-slit window.

'Begging your pardon, sir,' said Fowlstrangler, 'but this poor brain of mine can't judge so well between a lady and a window-box.' As the Baron prised loose his fingers and dropped him all the beetling height of the tower into the moat, his words dwindled down to a wet full stop: 'Them's both quite
pretty
your
lordship!'

Sobbing with frustration and pique, the Baron Greefenbludd hurled himself on to the bridal bed – and was greatly disconcerted, not to say bruised, to find bedsprings where he had fully expected a goosedown mattress. Somehow his left arm became inextricably tangled in a spring. He gnashed his teeth on the flowers that dropped from the kidnapped window-box. After the night's excitement, he was quite worn out, and Greefenbludd fell fast asleep, hugging to his chest the window-box, watered with tears.

A pair of gallant and uniformed officers happened at dawn upon the wreckage of an inn in a peaceful and sheltered valley near their barracks. On the ruins stood a young woman of extraordinary loveliness, waving a handkerchief to summon help. They also managed to pull from the ruins the innkeeper and an assortment of shivering guests.

The whole sorry story was told. Miss Amelia Divine reported how she had seen a hideous, dwarf-like creature sawing through the props supporting the inn, and afterwards had seen him stealing away towards the mountain pass with a padlocked chest on his back. When a search discovered neither her beloved father nor her big-nosed sister, Amelia was certain that her poor unfortunate relations must have been in that benighted trunk.

The officers set off in hottest pursuit, picking their way through avalanches and mudslides, the valiant Miss Amelia riding in tandem behind one.

'You mean to say that you have never heard of the evil Baron Greefenbludd?' exclaimed the subaltern around whose waist Amelia clung. 'I don't wish to frighten you, Fräulein, but your poor dear relations could not have fallen into fouler hands, if they are indeed prisoners at Bäddeschløss Grange.'

In the shadow of Bäddeschløss's mildewed, gloomy walls lay the tombs and vaults of the Baron's ignoble ancestors. The gravestones leaned at crazy angles, and the marble charnel-houses were noisy with starlings. At the sound of hoofbeats, a distracted figure ran up from a vault and clung piteously to the black railings. In one hand was a bright yellow duster – otherwise the riders might never have seen her through the turbid mists. As they drew closer, they could make out the details of her dress and her large, looming nose. 'It's Evelyn! We have found her!' cried Amelia. 'Thanks be to . . .'

Just then they came across the kindly Reverend Lovegood Divine who had been set to dig graves. He had been digging graves for some ten or twelve hours now, and had achieved quite an entrenchment across the foggy graveyard. Into the hole fell the galloping rescuers. Amelia and the two officers joined the reverend gentleman, in the twinkling of an upended horse, and lay quite stunned and winded. Evelyn looked on in dismay, helpless, and her large nose dripped with sorrow. Her bright yellow duster fluttered sadly down from her hand, as she saw the owner of the Grange totter sleepily out of the house. He had a window-box cradled to his breast, but more remarkable, perhaps, was the large bedstead he lugged along behind him, complete with silk sheet and four trailing chains. Two hounds bounded at his heels.

'Aha!' he exclaimed, standing at the end of the hole in which Amelia lay. 'You came at last, in time for your wedding day, my dear! As soon as I can free my arm from this confounded bedspring, your kind father the vicar shall join our hands in marriage.'

'Never!' cried the vicar.

'Never!' cried the unwilling bride.

'Ah! You will think differently after an hour or two in my charming torture chamber! Or should I feed these pleasant young officers to my faithful hounds.'

'Oh no!' cried the vicar, though whether he was thinking of the torture chamber or the young men, he did not say.

'I submit,' said Amelia, who was of course thinking of the young men. 'I shall marry you – whoever you are – but you must set free my big-nosed sister and my kindly father and these two pleasant young men.'

'Ach, let them go, but let them leave on foot – and may the great Grinwald Beast of the Transylvanian Plain crunch on their bones. You, wife, are the only one who interests me. Devil take me, woman, but you fire me with an insane passion. Let me get a taste of that frock!'

But as he seized hold of her bodice laces and wound them around his fingers like spaghetti, a pawing hand emerged from the moat behind him and patted the grassy bank, feeling for a handhold.

Out of the water came Fowlstrangler – a Fowlstrangler somewhat altered in appearance, however, for some important parts were missing. His hair was straggled with pondweed, and his pockets were full of fish. His silty crutch dripped slime. 'Baron Greefenbludd, I've been thinking,' he said, as he pulled an eel from his lederhosen.

'Ah Fowlstrangler! Make yourself useful,' the Baron interrupted him. 'Disentangle this bed from my arm immediately and fetch up my bride out of that hole. Our marriage is about to begin!'

But Fowlstrangler was not feeling useful, for Fowlstrangler had been *thinking*. 'My eyes don't see well by candlelight. My ears don't hear well in the dark. These brains of mine can't tell a maiden from a window-box. When you put me together, sir, in your ancestral workshop, begging your pardon, sir, but it seems to me that you used some very inferior materials . . .In fact I say you're a cheapskate, second-rate builder of monsters, sir, and I've a mind to be avenged on you for making me with poor eyes and poor ears and poor brains. If it pleases you, Master.' And so saying, he fell on Baron Greefenbludd and, seizing him by the bedstead, picked him up and ran with him towards the moat.

But if you think that they fell in and drowned, weighed down by the bridal bedstead, you are sadly mistaken. For as master and servant struggled and tore at one another with teeth and claws and horrid curses, the Grinwald Beast came lumbering off the Transylvanian Plain and ate them, blood and bone. It left the indigestible bedstead standing on the drawbridge. Later, a peasant stole it and sold it as a souvenir to a passing tourist, along with Bäddeschløss Grange.

Amelia and her large-nosed sister, Evelyn, were married to the two young officers, of course, by their kindly father, the Reverend Lovegood Divine. They left Transylvania on the Orient Express, which in those days went out of its way to oblige.

Alas, such days are long gone.

* * *

'You think I'm going to fall for that one, fella?' said Virgil, sheltering his wife in a bear-like embrace. 'That's a wagon-load of hooey you been giving me.'

'Don't take my word for it, please,' said MCC, heaving the modern mattress off the bedstead's base of springs. 'If you would care to extract the bed-key – that's a sort of spanner, supplied for the adjusting of the springing, don't you know. Have you found it?'

Unwilling to be made still more a fool of, Virgil groped among the springs suspiciously, and the bed resounded like a harp plucked out of tune. With a clatter, Virgil found the bed-key.

'Note the words *Facut in Transylvania* which, being translated, you will find means "Made in Transylvania". The maker's name you will find stamped on the angle-iron securing the bed-head to the frame.'

'Virgil, think of it!' cried his wife, going down on hands and knees to sneeze among the fluffy dust. 'Make the man sell you the bed, Virgil! We can put it in the shop and . . . gosh all-mighty, honey! See here where the chains were joined on! See where they just been nipped off short?' (In her astonishment, Ailsa too went down on her hands and knees to look.) 'Buy the bed, Virgil! Gosh knows, you don't got to sleep in it!'

'I don't?'

'No! Just put it in the store with the story wrote out real nice – like on the Dracula film posters. And maybe we could get wax-works. D'you think we could get wax-works, honey?'

Virgil and MCC were, by this time, poring over the telephone directory for the name of a shipping company which would transport the bed from Povey's Antiquary to the comic shop off the Chicago freeway.

Ailsa wrapped the bed-key in tissue-paper for the couple to take away with them, and Virgil and Lindy-Ann left arm in arm shortly afterwards, laughing raucously and discussing the possibility of opening a museum of horror in the basement. MCC squared up the mattress, then dusted off his hands and shirt and said, 'Well, that's me out of a bed. I'd best find somewhere else to lay my head. Thanks for the job. Thanks for the cheese sandwiches. If I were you, Mrs Povey, I'd open up the books side of the business. Fiction, that's what they want. That's what everyone wants really. Isn't it?' And he headed for the door.

'Mr Berkshire, wait!' called Mrs Povey. 'The shipping company won't be coming for the bed till Wednesday. You could maybe stay till . . .'

'Oh but I couldn't sleep in it now. It's someone else's property. Paid for. That would be dishonest.'

'MCC!' called Ailsa, but though he turned back towards her, she could not find anything to say.

'Ah yes,' he said, as if reminded by the sight of her. He felt in his breast pocket and held out to her the lead soldier from the bric-à-brac shelf. 'Take it. Keep it,' he said brightly. 'A souvenir.'

'I don't want it!' she replied, with as much rudeness as she could muster. He shrugged, put it back into his pocket, and hurried off down the street in the direction of the library. Now and then, he broke his stride with an overarm googly or off-break or spinning delivery of some imaginary cricket ball.

Ailsa ran and stood on the edge of the pavement and watched him out of sight.

CHAPTER THIRTEEN

THE ONLY ANSWER

After a while, Ailsa went back into the shop and sat down on the *chaise longue*. Her mother clearly wanted to say something helpful, something comforting, for she kept clearing her throat and dusting pieces of furniture with the palm of her hand. Knowing it would not help in the least, Ailsa turned and, at random, pulled a book off the shelf so as to be unapproachable. It was a trick she had learned from MCC. The book had a green, cloth-bound cover stained black by all the hands that had held it. The spine was torn down at the top so that the title was completely obliterated and she had to open it at the title page to read, *The Man who came from Reading*. With her heart pumping the blood a little too fast through her head to make reading easy, she let the pages fall open where they would, and found herself looking at a dull page – no action, no dialogue – just a description.

HE HAD ON a green corduroy jacket worn bald in all the creases of elbow, armpit and round the button-holes, and an untied green bow tie snaked from under his collar. His white cricket flannels were colour-matched to his jacket by the long, oval grass stains on both knees. His suede shoes, too, were like a badly worn wicket, with a lot

> of dark, bare patches showing. His dark, curly hair had receded to that point which makes men look extra-intelligent and shows the veins in their foreheads when they are excited, and it curled directly into a short, dark beard which isolated his face from the paler skin in the open collar of his shirt.

'Mother. Read this,' she said, thrusting the open book at Mrs Povey and starting to pace up and down the shop in time to her heartbeat. It couldn't be. He existed. She had touched him. He had to exist. Other people had seen him. Other people had had their lives changed by him. She struggled to recall the different customers who had bought or not bought at MCC's bidding – the major, the engaged couple, the spoilt girl, the Americans, the man at the auction room. Where were they now? All gone? All untraceable? Who could she run to and demand proof of his existence? She bitterly regretted now refusing the gift of the lead soldier, for that, it seemed now, would have been some tangible evidence that just five minutes before a living, breathing man had stood in the shop and . . . A wave of panic deafened her for a while to the excited rattling of Mr Singh at the door. The catch had slipped and he could not get in, despite pushing against the glass with his forehead. In his arms was clasped the inlaid wooden box.

Trembling with an agonizing delight, Ailsa slipped the catch and Mr Singh tumbled into the shop. 'I opened it! I did! I did! I opened it with a hairpin and oh-so-delicate probing, probing,' and he prodded at the air with the very hairpin, as if it would open to them, all three, the secrets of the universe.

'Oh dear,' said Mrs Povey quietly to her daughter. 'I'm afraid poor dear MCC is found out. His "fictions" are about to be shown up for what they are.'

Immediately Ailsa dreaded the awful revelation of the

empty box and the complaints of the newsagent, cheated out of his money by a fast-talking storyteller.

But Mr Singh's face was wreathed in smiles. He had seen into the box already and now he pushed his hand in under the lid and pulled out a dull, dangling object which he thrust so close to Ailsa's face that she screamed. It was an old, decaying, half-wound plait of hair, its original colour lost . . . as were the markings of the dead snake coiled up in the bottom of the box along with a nib pen and some brown, crumbling sheets of writing paper. 'The bicycle-riding young gentleman's story was all true!' he said, with a look which apologized for any slight doubt he had harboured. 'Where he is? I want to show him inside this very delightful box.'

Ailsa turned triumphantly on her mother who had just read and thrown aside the green-bound book. 'You see! He didn't tell lies at all! His stories were all true, Mother! Look at the bed! "Made in Transylvania" and the chains just nipped off short! He didn't tell lies. He just knew an awful lot, that's all.'

'No. That's not it, my dear.' Mrs Povey pointed at the book where it lay on the floor, the exact colour and texture of MCC Berkshire's shoes. 'MCC Berkshire doesn't exist, my dear.'

'But his stories!'

'Are true. Yes. And if Mr Berkshire doesn't exist but we know his stories for true, there is only one explanation.' She walked away, too overwhelmed by the momentousness of her discovery to let them share it, and when she shut the door of the living room, her movements beyond it made not a sound. Ailsa turned to find Mr Singh gone too, the door sighing itself shut without a single ring from the bell under the mat.

She bent to look out of the window, and the oblong of April sky she could see had turned a peculiar white. Flocks of migrating birds arriving with the spring flew in dense, straight lines overhead like typed words on a sheet of paper. She repeated what her mother had said, although the words seemed unable to escape her mouth as she spoke them, and a strange blankness seemed to be seeping into her brain. 'If MCC doesn't exist, but we know his stories for true, there is only one explanation.'

Realization fell on her not like a ray of light or a clap of thunder but like a white dust-sheet settling very gradually over a piece of old furniture.

Michael Charles Christie Berkshire drew the sheet of paper out of his typewriter with a shuddering sigh and laid it face down on top of the others, pinning it in place with a single lead toy soldier. Behind him, beyond the sun-filled open window, a shout went up – an appeal for lbw – and a polite patter of applause said that another batsman's innings was over. Only a friendly village match, only the Reading Second Eleven, but the first of the season.

Not that Michael was ever asked to play. Oh, they told him he was 'in reserve' so that he sat all day in cricket flannels in his bedroom overlooking the pitch, but he was never called on to play. He wished people would not humour him like that. Of course they wanted players who could see the ball to hit it. And run.

He patted around the desk-top until he found his glasses, and put them on. The comforts of his room swam into view – the shabby furniture, the hundreds of books, the box-files full of manuscripts only waiting for the day he became a famous and sought-after author. But his heart continued to ache.

Downstairs in the kitchen, his mother was making sandwiches for the cricketers' tea, and their neighbour was once again lending the benefit of her advice in a stream of well-meaning prattle.

'The trouble is, he doesn't get out enough, shut away in that room all day – even in this lovely weather – rattling away at that typewriter – we can hear it, you know, right through the wall – three, four o'clock in the morning. I mean he's never going to find a girlfriend, sitting in his room all day, is he? You should make him go out – take him out of himself it would. There's plenty of plain girls in the world wouldn't sneeze at him despite his . . .'

'He's very shy,' said his mother's voice in an apologetic murmur. 'He's got his books. So long as he's happy.'

'Yes, but scribbling stories all day! That doesn't bring in any money, does it? That doesn't help you with the housekeeping – and you a widow trying to manage. He's just a drain on you, that's what. It's not fair. It was the same when he was at school, my Johnnie says. None of the other kids could make head nor tail of him; said he was always fibbing – telling whoppers, anyway. No wonder they ragged him – cruel, but what else can you expect? And there's my Johnnie married and with kids of his own and a Ford Sierra. And what's going to become of your Michael, that's what I wonder? It's only friendly concern makes me say it, but he ought to get out more . . . make some friends . . . make himself useful at least . . .'

Michael Charles Christie Berkshire pushed the typewriter away from him and stood up and stamped. The circulation always packed up in his bad leg when he had sat for a long time. He caught sight of himself in the mirror, his eyes shrunken to piggy little smudges by the grotesque thickness of the glasses. His sparse, mousy hair was stuck to his pallid head with the sweat of concentration. That drawn, sickly face in the mirror was like the glimpse of an old enemy across the room at a party – someone he had spent years trying to avoid.

He pulled on his old green corduroy jacket and felt better at once. Wasn't at least the little lead soldier, standing on his finished typescript, saluting him respectfully? 'I had to leave, though, didn't I? I couldn't stay for ever!' said Michael aloud. 'They got away from me. My characters. I lost control of them. You heard them: they were working it all out! They got too real for me!'

No, perhaps after all the soldier was beckoning rather than saluting: some strange, crooked gesture.

'I mean I can't go back, can I?' cried Michael, and the pain in his heart was momentarily much greater than the pain in his leg. 'It's all just made-up lies!' he suddenly shouted at the little lead soldier. 'I'm just a damnable liar! Aren't I?'

A breeze from the open window dislodged the top few sheets of typing and toppled the lead soldier on to his back. Michael scrabbled clumsily to save the whole stack from being scattered around the room, finishing on his hands and knees, putting the pages in order again. His eye ran over a sentence here, a paragraph there.

'Of course I could always change the ending,' he said, absent-mindedly slipping the soldier into his breast pocket. 'Perhaps it would work better if I just changed the last few . . . That's it! That's what I'll do! I'll do it!' And the ache in his chest immediately subsided as he sat down at the desk again and pulled his typewriter towards him.

When the last cricketer was out, and the last uneaten cucumber sandwiches had been left deserted along the trestle-tables, Mrs Berkshire mustered them together on to a single plate. She could hear the rattle and ting of a typewriter overhead, and climbed the stairs to her son's bedroom. 'Would you like to finish these up?' she began, putting her head around the door. But the bedroom was empty. 'That's strange. I could have sworn . . . How could he have come by me without me seeing? Still . . . it's good for him to get out. I'm glad. I'm glad.'

She went to tidy the desk, and took a quick, incurious glance at the title of her son's latest little 'effort'. 'Oh, I don't think that's a very nice title, Michael,' she thought primly, crossly. And separating the one sheet from the rest, she tore up the title page of *A Pack of Lies* and dropped it into the wastepaper basket.

From the bottom of the bin, a circular shine caught her eye, and she bent down with a gasp of relief to snatch up (from among a few torn sheets) Michael's glasses. So nearly lost!

'But oh! where could he possibly have gone without these?' she said to herself.